THE
Pursuit
OF
Michelle

WILLIAM RYMER

PAGE PUBLISHING, INC.
Conneaut Lake, PA

First originally published by Page Publishing 2021

ISBN 978-1-6624-6183-5 (pbk)
ISBN 978-1-6624-6185-9 (digital)

Printed in the United States of America

CHAPTER 1

Michelle sat quietly at her table, listening to the sounds of a house band and soaking in some much-needed "me time" while consuming several mixed drinks. Michelle's body swayed back and forth while her foot tapped to the rhythm of drums and guitars playing oldies but goodies. She took much time earlier preparing herself for the night out by soaking in a warm bath, paying extra attention to her hair and makeup, and slipping into a sexy yellow dress with black thigh-high pantyhose and black high heels. Michelle's dress was low-centered over her breast, which was impressively large and well-rounded while deciding to be a little naughty and leave the panties at home tonight. She was what men called "a looker" because of the features she presented and how many men look multiple times as she walked by and caught the scent of her Love Spell body spray. Her hair was brunette with light-colored highlights. with striking brown eyes and a mouth that looked like it could suck forever and never lose its sexy form. She possessed large, amazing breasts with an ass you wanted to sink every inch into and never pull out of when unloading. Michelle was not the commitment kind but could fuck a man so good he would want to divorce his wife and beg for her body.

Michelle was rolling her orange-painted fingernail around the top of her glass and was beginning to feel a warm rush of alcohol pushing through her body while stimulating her need to break loose and sing. While mumbling the words to a Def Leppard song, she observed a younger couple sitting across from her and watched how they interacted. She observed the young girl was in her mid-twenties as well as the man and noticed the girl seemed to be cold-shouldering the young man. The young woman was attractive, but the man had features that any woman would find stimulating. As the music broke and could hear much talking within the area, Michelle, nosing, overheard the woman saying she was tired and wanted him to call her a cab.

The young man kept his composure and said, "Excuse me, I need to run to the bathroom."

As the young man walked away, Michelle observed her calling another person and asking if they wanted to hookup because she was not into the man she was dating and trying to break it off. Michelle could not understand why she would not be into the attractive, well-mannered, and gentleman-approached man.

Michelle pondered the moment and decided to take a bold move. She stood up, walked over to the table, and asked if she could sit down.

The young woman asked, "Who the fuck are you?"

Michelle responded, "Look, bitch, here is twenty dollars, call a fucking cab and leave."

The young woman looked amazed and snatched the twenty from her hand and said "Fuck you" while heading out the door.

Michelle had always possessed a man's approach from the other way; she decided she would be something different and show this young man what a woman can do for him. As Michelle began to drink her drink, the young man returned and said, "Sorry, I must be confused and went to the wrong table."

Michelle responded, "No, you are at your table. I have decided to join you, do you mind?"

The young man hesitated for a second and quickly said "No, ma'am" and sat down. He was stunned by her beauty while being confused as to what just happened.

"Look," said Michelle, "my name is Michelle, and I overheard the interaction between you and your date and stepped in and bought her a cab."

The young man replied, "Do I know you?"

Michelle looked at him and said, "No, but would you like to?"

He began to stutter his words, finally gained control, and said, "Sorry, my name is Xavier."

Michelle reached out her hand to shake his and said, "Nice to meet you, Xavier."

Xavier was dumbfounded and tried his hardest to keep his eyes focused on her pretty face without dropping them to observe her large breasts. He became curious as he watched Michelle speak about who she was and how she conjured up the courage to walk over and kick out his date so she could sit with him. Once, Michelle stuck her finger in her mouth and sucked off the excess alcohol she rubbed off from the rim of her drink, leaving him in a state of amazement. Xavier became more and more attracted to her mentally and physically as the short talk became a more profound, intellectual, conversational exchange. He began to understand she possessed not only beauty but a significant amount of intelligence that he found exhilarating and almost breathtaking.

Why would this early-thirty attractive woman want a young guy in his later twenties? thought Xavier. He noticed how she moved her body to the beat of the music while exchanging personals between them. He interrupted her and said, "Sorry, I find you extremely attractive and would like nothing more than to dance."

Michelle gladly stood as he reached his hand out to her and invited her to the dance floor.

Xavier confessed he had never danced and did not know why he asked her to dance but was drawn by her beauty to be close to her by dancing.

Michelle smiled and said, "I'm a great teacher and don't mind showing you."

Xavier was almost to the point of passing out because every ounce of blood was quickly rushing to his cock in which he pleaded sincerely not to show itself at this time. Michelle showed him how to hold hands and position their bodies while placing his hand onto her hip area. Xavier felt the smoothness of her skin and putting his hand on her hip drove him into a deeper state of erotic attraction than any other time in his life. He became lost in her eyes as she began to swing to the music's beat and watching her lips move and instruct his movement became soothing and almost heavenly. Michelle became flushed with warmth as she pressed her body next to his and began to feel a tingle deep inside her body that was begging to take him right at this moment. She laid her head on his neck area and felt Xavier moving his hand up and down her side while holding her a little tighter as the song played. Xavier could feel her hair's softness and caught a scent of her perfume in which he found pleasing.

The next song was slow and romantic. Xavier turned Michelle's body backward and placed her back up against his chest while wrapping his arms around her waist. Michelle became a little embarrassed but overflowing with desire as she felt his cock bulging against her ass. She leaned her head back onto his shoulder and looked the other way, allowing her hand to run up to his head and pressing his warm lips onto the exposure of her neck. Michelle gripped his hands around her body tightly and pressed her beautiful ass up against his dick while feeling the warmth of his lips searching her soft neck. She quickly spun around and looked at his eyes, which were attractively blue, and slowly pressed her lips against his and passionately made out for several seconds in a deep, blissful position. As their lips found each other, their mouths slightly opened, and Michelle felt the softness of his tongue touching hers, which sent pulses down her body like never before. Xavier lowered his head slightly to her ear with a light bite and asked if he could take her somewhere more private.

Michelle looked at him and said, "Please."

Michelle turned and began to walk back toward his table while overflowing with sexual tension. Xavier followed close behind and observed her hourglass figure and how her nicely rounded ass created a work of art down to her crafted legs. Xavier found the middle-aged goddess charming and delightfully appealing and wanted to know more about her than any other girl in his dating history. Michelle grabbed her purse and asked where he would like to go.

Xavier replied, "I have a confession, so I live in the guesthouse at my parents while I plan to establish a dream home on the back side of our property."

Michelle thought for a second and said, "I admire your honesty. Do not be ashamed of who you are or where you live while trying to make a better future."

Xavier was relieved to hear Michelle's kind and understanding words but loaned to have a nice place where he could take a date. Michelle quickly replied, "Let's go to my place."

Xavier said, "No, I want to show you where I live and who I am."

CHAPTER 2

Xavier walked with Michelle across the street to his older '74 Chevy truck and opened the door that sent off a high-pitched creak. Xavier again appeared embarrassed. Michelle was no stranger to men taking her places in high-end cars and pounding her pussy on $2,000 leather seats. Still, Michelle found Xavier different and realized he was genuine with a lot of realism she found attractive. Michelle hopped up into his truck and caught a scent of an older vehicle and observed several items, such as small tools, bookwork, and a shirt within the seat. Xavier closed his door and asked Michelle if she was ready to go.

Michelle responded, "Yes, and by the way, I love this truck."

Xavier was pleased with Michelle's approval of his vehicle and explained his grandfather had left the truck for him as a part of his will and meant a lot to him. Michelle began to become weaker, wetter, and almost falling for a man she just met. As Xavier started the vehicle and began driving down the dimly lit streets, Michelle was overly aroused and wanted to drop her head in his lap and suck every drop of his balls. She chewed on the side of her jaw and would repeatedly squeeze her legs together, feeling warmth, wetness, and a tingling sensation of being sexually aroused. She kept her composure and withheld her desire to provoke him at this time but wrestled with her thoughts, *You are a grown woman. Go for it.*

Michelle withheld her desire to sexually provoke the moment even though she found the whole experience different and overwhelmingly exciting, making her feel young again. They traveled for several minutes through town and then into the suburbs while turning onto a dirt road and a bit bumpy, leading up to a farmstyle home. Xavier parked his truck in front of a guesthouse left of the main house and approached Michelle's side of the door while once again revealing the loud squeak of the opening door in which Michelle replied, "Don't worry about it, the truck has character."

Xavier once again asked Michelle if she would like to come inside his home for a while. Michelle said yes, and as they entered, she felt a warm feeling and noticed the guesthouse was homey and had a dimly lit fire in the fireplace. Xavier ran around quickly, trying to pick up his clothes around his bachelor's pad.

Xavier yelled out, "Can I make you a drink?"

Michelle responded, "A Jack with Coke would be fine."

Xavier popped his head around the corner and said, "Sorry, I have the Coke but not the Jack. I'm not much of a drinker, but I can run next door and grab you a Bud Light from the garage."

Michelle smiled while running her fingers through her hair, pulling it over her ear, saying, "That sounds good."

Michelle found Xavier's nervousness attractive and could not believe how she has lost focus on how a man could want to please her without going straight to fucking or pushing her onto her knees to enjoy her mouth. She sat there and thought for a moment while Xavier ran around the house quickly and reflected on how a man would have her spread by now on his bed or feeling her warm mouth sucking his load out of his dick without any interaction and just sex. Michelle discovered she had fallen into a routine that was sexually satisfying but lacked all personal interactions; just last week, she remembered going back to her date's home, and before she sat on his sofa, she had already been bent over and fucked over his kitchen counter. Most would say she acted like a whore, but she was an adult, liked men and dick, and had learned to skip the geriatrics and went straight for the sex without personalization. Michelle remembered when one of her dates was ejaculating in her pussy from behind, she caught a glimpse of a family picture on the wall, revealing he had a wife and information he did not share or did she ask. Fucking had become a go-to for stress relief and an outlet for self-pleasure.

Michelle overheard the side door close and watched with laughter as Xavier was moving too fast and tripped over a pool toy trying to retrieve a beer for her. She realized no one has worked this hard for her in many years and was intrigued by his willingness to please her. Michelle noticed a shirt beside her on the sofa, and she picked it up and could smell the odor of his cologne that was well-pleasing to her senses. She laid it back down as she noticed Xavier was crossing back across the pool area while holding her beer. Xavier stopped and sat her beer on the poolside table and lit the candle while turning on the colored waterfall that flowed into the pool. He approached her in the house and asked if she would join him by the pool on this beautiful night while holding out his hand. Michelle was stunned by how proper he was approaching her. He could have fucked her twice by now, and she would have been okay with that, but his eagerness to please her and impress her was amazingly attractive. She gripped his nervous hand and followed him to the pool area table and kicked off the high heels as they began to talk and become familiar within a more intimate environment.

The lights flickered across the pool water as the night sky twinkled with bright stars. Michelle learned a lot about Xavier and how he was raised in the country and had set goals to become an accomplished journalist. Xavier watched Michelle as they spoke, and he continued to grab her a couple more beers. As her legs were crossed, he noticed her thigh-high pantyhose that sent waves of arousal and increased his heart rate, sending extreme amounts of blood to his penis. He explained how he had learned to work a farm and had failed to find acceptable dates that were more down to home. Michelle felt a little embarrassed because she had every intention to fuck and enjoy his young stud penis for a night with all purposes for just sex.

Xavier is excellent, thought Michelle, and even though he has not tried to induce her sexually, she was willing and waiting for the moment to make it happen. Michelle intentionally knocked over her beer onto her dress and added much drama saying, "Oh no, look at what my clumsiness has done."

Xavier quickly retrieved a towel and tried to help her clean up the beer on the table and dress. He helped her wipe up the spilled beer while noticing beer had splashed onto her breast, revealing a sexy glitter of sparkle. He offered her to come in, and he would wash her dress for her. Michelle asked if she could take a shower.

Xavier said, "By all means, please help yourself." Xavier walked Michelle to the back of his home while crossing through his bedroom.

Michelle felt a tickle run through her body down to her pussy as she passed by his bed and thought about how she wanted to be spread and fucked hard on his sheets. Xavier turned on the shower and grabbed one of his clean shirts from his closet for Michelle to wear while he prepared to wash her dress.

Michelle said, "Thank you, I'm sorry to be so much trouble."

He replied with a smile and said, "I'm happy to help, and let me know if you need anything and just hang your dress on the other side of the door, and I will take care of it."

Michelle slowly unbuttoned her dress after Xavier walked out and closed the door while dropping it to the floor and standing there with nothing on but her sexy thigh-high black pantyhose. She reached for the door and started to turn the knob while opening it slightly with intentions to invite Xavier into her hot shower. She stopped and closed her eyes and slowly closed the door, wondering and asking herself if this was what she should do to a guy who had his entire future before him, and if she fucked him, he will more than likely fall in love. Michelle dropped her pantyhose and hung her dress outside the door. She stepped into the shower and began to feel the warm water trickle over her body and drip off her ample breast while her pussy burned with the desire to fuck. She pondered the decision to yell out for him but was afraid he would identify her as a loose woman trying to catch an excellent one-night stand with this gentleman.

"Is this not why we came back to his house but to fuck?" Michelle battled with her desires as she began to rub her body. She found herself fingering her pussy and sending waves of sexual pleasure throughout her body as she stroked her hardened clit faster and faster. Michelle stopped and placed both hands on the shower wall, gained control of her desires, and meditated to calm her sexual drive to a more manageable level.

Michelle's mind would not stop going in so many directions, and she started to imagine him outside the shower door tightly gripping his hard cock while vigorously stroking at the thought of her naked body in his shower. She imagined him straining and yelling as he sprayed his load onto the outside of the glass shower door, and the image of his warm white load trickling down the glass sent extreme sexual tension throughout her body. Michelle jumped like a teenager in trouble as Xavier knocked on the door, asking if she was okay and needed anything.

She nervously replied, "I'm good, thanks."

Xavier continued to say, "Please help yourself to my room. My shirt is lying on the bed."

Michelle replied, "Thank you, I'm sorry to be so much trouble."

Xavier said, walking away, "No trouble at all."

Michelle stepped out of the steamy shower and dried her hair and body while walking out naked into Xavier's room. She walked around with the empowerment of being nude and laying for a few minutes on his bed and observing his decor. She stood in front of his mirror and tried on his tight shirt around her large breast while lifting the length and revealing her darkened pubic hairs.

CHAPTER 3

Michelle caught the scent of Xavier's body spray and found the odor peacefully while continuing to walk around his personal space. While standing in front of his dresser, she noticed an assortment of trophies and accomplishments he had earned from high school. His wall contained several comic hero posters, figures, and models she found interesting. While looking out his window, his view consisted of a mass field dimly lit by the moonlight and black figures that appeared to be herds of cattle. At that moment, she heard a knock and quickly ran over to the bedroom door while slightly opening it to find Xavier asking if she was okay and would she like to join him for dinner.

Michelle said, "It's okay. We do not have to run back out for dinner. I can grab something later."

Xavier replied, "Oh no, I have thrown a small dinner together, and it would be my pleasure to have dinner with you. Will you join me?"

Michelle was surprised; most of her dates would take her to a nice dinner to impress her and immediately take her to their car, home, or any surface that would allow them to get off onto her body. She replied, "I would love to have dinner with you, and do you have a pair of shorts I could borrow?" At that moment, through unintentional interaction, Xavier caught sight of Michelle's nice, rounded ass in his bedroom mirror directly behind her and became a little nervous.

"Yes, uh, yea, I will go and see if I can find you some shorts," said Xavier.

A couple of minutes later, Xavier knocked on the door and slightly opened the door while pushing a pair of his red university shorts into the room with Michelle.

"Thank you," said Michelle. She slipped the shorts on and had to tie them up so they would not fall off onto the flooring. As Michelle exited the bedroom, she caught a scent of food that smelled like grilled cheese. She approached the kitchen area and noticed Xavier with a towel over his shoulder standing in front of the stove.

"There you are. Do you like grilled cheese?"

Michelle responded, "Why, yes, it has been a long time since I have eaten a grilled cheese, but that sounds great."

Xavier turned to her and said, "You are pretty, and I love the shorts."

Michelle blushed and thanked Xavier as she sat down at the table. She was accustomed to men exclaiming how hot she was or how sexy she looked, but the word he used saying she was pretty made her feel more attractive than any other comment within her past because it seemed natural and genuine.

"Sorry, I do not have much to choose from considering dinner options. I eat a lot of TV dinners and small things that are quick. If the grilled cheese is not suitable for you, I will gladly run out and grab you something of your choice."

Michelle looked at his smile and perfect white teeth and agreed the dinner looked great and couldn't wait to try his cooking.

Xavier placed a steaming plate containing a grilled cheese in front of Michelle and asked her if she would like Coke, water, another beer, or grape juice.

Michelle said, "You know, no more drinks tonight, but I would love to try a Coke."

Xavier grabbed a glass, dropped some ice that created a clinging sound, and poured her some fresh Coke right out of the can while the sizzling sounds filled the room. He handed her the glass while

Michelle said thank you and glanced at him in his eyes. Michelle grabbed the hot grilled cheese, took a bite, and expressed how pleasing the taste was and how she had not eaten one in years. Xavier was pleased he cooked food that Michelle enjoyed and peeked at her often as she ate her food. He found her extremely attractive but was confused about what direction he should move toward while trying not to mess up the current situation.

Should I make a move? Is this not why we came here, or should we just talk? thought Xavier. "What do you like to do for fun?" asked Xavier.

Michelle took a small drink and thought for a moment. "Well, I mostly work a lot and love to work out, but fun, I do not know. Sorry, I'm a little boring."

Xavier said, "Boring? I think you are beautiful and funny."

Michelle blushed and asked, "What do you do for a living, if I may ask?"

Xavier responded, "I'm a freelance reporter for our local news."

Michelle smiled and said, "Wow, impressive."

"You want to do something fun?" said Xavier.

"What might that be?" said Michelle, who has become exceedingly curious.

"If you look outside, I have a vast amount of land we can ride a four-wheeler on and would love for you to take a late-night ride with me through the country," said Xavier.

Michelle quickly said, "I have not ridden a four-wheeler, but that sounds fun, let's do it."

Michelle continued to eat and ponder the course of the evening. She reflected on how her traditional dates involved upper-end dinners and extreme sexual contact, usually close to after dinner or even before leaving the parking lot. The urban environment she was accustomed to had become riddled with quick dinners and hard fucking that involved almost no personal interactions. Just last week, Michelle met a man at a local bookstore down on Twenty-Ninth Street, and while small talking over a book, they went to grab at the same time ended up with her on her knees in the bathroom performing oral sex and swallowing his load while he aggressively pulled her hair. Once, she went out with a man she met within a restaurant who asked to buy her a drink while the evening ended up with her spread wide in his car, taking his dick deep inside of her in the passenger seat and exploding all over her belly and breasts. Michelle was intrigued at how Xavier has not made a move, especially when she was wet and willing.

As dinner finished up and Michelle thanked Xavier for the food, Xavier asked if she was ready. Michelle said, "Are you serious? We are going to ride in the dark out in the country and with a man I barely know?"

Nervously Xavier pleaded that he was sorry.

Michelle said, "I'm joking. It sounds fun."

Michelle and Xavier walked out to a barn directly behind his house and entered the structure. Michelle could smell the sweet smell of straw and animal feed. As she caught sight of a fresh pile of straw, she said out loud, "Have you ever just jumped into the straw and rolled around?"

Xavier pushed the four-wheeler out and walked back in and said, "That has happened many times and is fun." Xavier reached out his hand and said, "Jump with me into the pile."

Michelle smiled and said, "Really?"

"Yes," said Xavier.

Michelle grabbed his hand, feeling like a teenager, and they moved forward and jumped into the pile and began to roll around and giggle while throwing straw high into the air. Michelle has straw all in her hair as they continued to throw it up into the air and try to stuff straw into each other's clothing. Xavier forgot that Michelle was dressed only in his shirt and shorts with his socks and pulled her shirt too far open from the top and caught a nice look at her breasts' cleavage. Michelle looked and laughed at Xavier, pulling her shirt back and jokingly saying, "No, no, mister, not second base yet."

They both fell into the pile of hay while Michelle landed on top of Xavier with her chest against his and her legs spread open over his right leg. Xavier paused and stared into Michelle's brown eyes, ran his right hand through her messed-up hair, and pulled her head toward him closer. Both gazed deep into each other's eyes and slowly pressed their lips onto each other and passionately kissed deeply while working each tongues slowly in and out of each other's mouths. Xavier took his left hand and rubbed lightly down Michelle's side, feeling her perfect hourglass shape curve while pulling Michelle's hair back slightly, revealing her neck and biting her so slightly. Xavier pulled Michelle close to his body and gave her a soft hug and asked her if she wanted to take a ride now.

Michelle gazed for a second at Xavier and quietly inside said, *Are you fucking kidding me, fuck me now.* She replied, "Sure, let's take a ride."

Michelle lifted her body from the straw. Simultaneously, Xavier prepared the ATV. She was dumbfounded about why he had rejected all sexual advances, especially when she was almost naked, barely covered in his clothing. Michelle was not accustomed to rejection and liked what she liked and was used to men going great distances to achieve her position on her knees or spread wide for their pleasure. She continued to examine what she has done and if something was wrong with her. Xavier started the ATV, and Michelle could feel the sound vibrating and caught the scent of burning fuel.

Xavier turned his head back to Michelle and said, "Would you like a ride?"

Within Michelle's thoughts, she deeply agreed with the invention and a sexual approach that involved her on her knees and being mounted from behind in the straw. Michelle was pouting a little, walked over the ATV, placed her hand on Xavier's shoulder, and mounted the four-wheeler behind his sitting position while wrapping her hands around his waist area.

Xavier rived the throttle, and Michelle enjoyed the raw power and vibrations just under her ass area. He started to roll forward slowly while exiting the barn and turned toward a path leading to a field. Michelle could feel the cool breeze flowing through her hair and held tightly as the ATV bounced and rolled over bumps and rough areas. Xavier turned his head slightly and said, "Are you ready?"

Michelle responded, "Ready for what?"

Xavier brought the ATV to a stop, and Michelle was trying to look around and figure out what she was preparing for or about the experience. Xavier placed his left hand on Michelle's tightly joined hand and said, "This."

Michelle let out a scream of excitement as Xavier punched the throttle and began speeding down the path. She felt every bump and vibration that sent excitement through her body. Her hair was flying everywhere and caught slight chills flowing down her shirt and stimulating her bare breast. Xavier moved the ATV through the path with his dimly lit headlight and knew every turn and bump as they approached a slight downward grade of terrain. Michelle caught sight of the moon illuminating a creek. Xavier speedily hit the water, causing water to splash upward and onto their bodies. Michelle burst out in excitement and screamed while she felt cool water running down her back and began to experience no worries within this moment as she gazed at Xavier's face while wrapping her hands even tighter around his waist and laying her head on his shoulder.

CHAPTER 4

Michelle was a little cold but satisfied by the onset of the warmth Xavier's back provided. Every so often, the ATV would hit a bump, sending Michelle's body bouncing up and down. She quickly let go of her sexual tension from the barn and enjoyed the moment and thought why she had never experienced such a thrilling event. Michelle was starting to feel an attachment and almost need to know Xavier personally and realized this evening was the best experience she has had in a long while. At that moment, Michelle felt the ATV slowing and coming to a stop atop a big hill they had been climbing for a time. Xavier stepped off the ATV and helped Michelle while offering to carry her to avoid her walking in the high grass without shoes. Michelle was intrigued and allowed Xavier to pick her up and hold her close while walking toward a path.

Michelle asked, "Where are you taking me?"

Xavier said, "I want to show you something."

As the path foliage began to thin, Michelle caught sight of a wooden bench just ahead. Xavier lowered her gently and sat beside her on the bench. Xavier said, "Look out toward the hillside."

Michelle saw a hillside with a waterfall trickling down the grade and pouring into a small body of water. Xavier explained he planned to build his dream home on the hill facing the waterfall and often imagined him with a wife and children playing throughout the area. Michelle became a little nervous and felt she could never be that person or experience life with one man or have children, but the thought was pleasing and comforting.

The moonlight highlighted the waterfall. Michelle could hear the water falling directly into the larger body of water and started to imagine a house on the side of the hill and what life would be like leaving an urban environment while residing in a country setting.

"Do you hear that?" said Xavier.

"Hear what?" said Michelle.

"Exactly that," said Xavier. Xavier continued to explain how you see or hear no traffic, honks, or people talking, just peaceful countryside sounds. Michelle was accustomed to an urban environment and lacked the privilege to sit and take in such beautiful sights.

"Are you cold?" asked Xavier.

Michelle responded, "Just a little, I'm okay."

Xavier stood up, pulled off his long-sleeve shirt and handed it to Michelle, asking her to please put it on to relieve her from the cold. Michelle felt a tickle deep inside her pussy as she caught the sight of Xavier's bare chest and noticed how his body was not very big but looked fit with muscle tone and abs that rolled down to his pants. Michelle felt horny and wanted more than anything to run her tongue over his body and find her way to his cock. She quickly discovered her imagination developing a scene that involved him pulling her shirt up and deeply sucking her breast as she positioned her body over his cock and gliding it into her pussy. To her surprise, he placed his arm around her shoulder and caressed her body while rubbing her back to supply warmth.

Xavier explained how he had enjoyed the evening and must head back to his home due to his early commitment in the morning. As Xavier once again carried her back to the ATV and placed her on the seat, Michelle went for a kiss and felt Xavier respond willingly. Michelle rubbed her hand on the back of his neck and opened her legs while pulling his body close to her body as she sat on the ATV and he stood just over her. Xavier's kissing quickly became passionate, and his hands began finding their way under Michelle's shirt, rubbing the small of her back. Michelle started to burn with passion as Xavier placed his hand on the side of her leg and sucked hard on her neck. She pushed her body forward and could feel his cock inside his pants, placing pressure against her vagina area. Her hands rubbed his entire bare back area while her mouth found its way to his chest area. Xavier let out a gentle moan as Michelle lightly bit his chest area. Xavier grabbed Michelle's hips, pulled her onto his body while standing, and placed his tongue deep into her mouth. At the same time, Michelle willingly participated and grinded her vaginal area against his cock. Xavier stopped and tightly wrapped his hands around Michelle and stated they needed to stop.

Michelle responded, "No, it's okay."

Xavier said, "Please, I must stop and take you back home."

Michelle positioned her body just behind Xavier once again on the ATV and began riding the trail back toward his home. She was upset, frustrated, and pondering why this man had not jumped her body and used her for sexual pleasure. Michelle did not give up quickly, and as the ride continued, she slowly slipped her hand onto his crotch area and began rubbing his penis. She started to apply ample amounts of pleasure, trying to gain his attention; she felt him accepting her invention to rub his area and asked him to pull over. Xavier stopped the ATV just before crossing the water and killed the engine. Michelle became excited about the possibility she had accomplished her mission and was about to feel his rod enter portions of her body.

Xavier climbed off the ATV and stood close to Michelle and said, "I think you are beautiful and unique. I would like to get to know you a little better before considering contact on a deeper level."

Michelle responded, "I'm sorry, it's been a wonderful evening; I have not had this much fun in years, and I'm physically drawn to you. Please forgive me if I have gone too far."

Xavier placed both his hands on each side of her face and gave her a small, passionate kiss and said, "Let's take this a little slow and get to know each other."

Xavier restarted the ATV and asked Michelle if she was ready. Michelle said "No, it's cold" and let out a scream of excitement as Xavier once again charged the throttle and splashed the water high in the air. The air ran over Michelle's once again wet body and became an incredible feeling. She tried to calm down and was pouting a little from the rejection and introduction to the first man who did not want to explore her body sexually. Michelle had already planned to give this man anything he wanted, but the rejection has forced her to reevaluate her intentions and interactions of the night. Michelle laid her head on the back of Xavier, and as she calmed her frustration, she absorbed his warmth and enjoyed the feeling of his company and the excitement of the evening. Confused, sexually frustrated, and treading in new territory, Michelle began to think about how men have treated her over the years as they finished the trail ride to the barn's destination. As Xavier pulled the ATV into the barn, he spun the tires, giving a force of vibrations that could be felt deep in the seat that had become a comforting feeling for Michelle. Michelle watched as Xavier began to cover the ATV and thought of how he was gentle and such a gentleman to her and wondered if he would want to see her beyond their evening.

Xavier turned from the ATV and extended his hand, asking Michelle if she would like to stay the night at his home. Michelle considered the offer because it was Friday and no other commitments and became excited that he wanted to continue the evening.

"Absolutely, I would like that," said Michelle.

Michelle and Xavier walked back into his small home, and Michelle sat on the sofa facing the fire Xavier had prepared. She could feel the warmth and hear the sounds of the wood popping and crackling.

Xavier asked, "Would you like a new set of clothing?"

Michelle responded, "Yes, that would be great. My outfit is a little damp."

Xavier walked into the bedroom and scrambled through his drawers until he found a blue-colored flannel shirt, shorts, and some long white socks. "I hope this is sufficient," said Xavier.

Michelle said, "It's perfect."

Xavier responded, "Please help yourself to the bedroom, and would you like a nice cup of tea?"

Michelle almost laughed. she had the thought of *Tea?* Most men would be gagging her on her knees at this point with their hardened dick instead of offering tea or pounding her deeply on the sofa instead of offering tea. "That sound's great," said Michelle, trying to understand the intentions of the night. She walked into the bedroom and dropped all her clothing while standing once again naked in his bedroom.

Michelle slipped on his socks and noticed how baggy they formed while pulling his blue shirt onto her body. Michelle buttoned the shirt while looking in the mirror and stopped halfway and wanted to leave a little sight of her cleavage to entice Xavier. Once again, Michelle could smell the odor of Xavier's cologne within his clothing, and the smell stimulated her intensely throughout her body, sending pulses of desire to every inch of her body. She ran her fingers through her hair while teasing it to gain a sexy texture and applied a little makeup, trying to accomplish her desire to attract Xavier. Michelle opened the door and saw the environment darkened with the twinkle of fire, their remaining only light source. She noticed Xavier sitting on the sofa while preparing a couple of glasses on the coffee table.

Xavier looked at Michelle and said, "Wow, you look nice in my clothing."

Michelle was enticed that Xavier commented on her appearance and sat next to him on the sofa while sitting with her legs crossed, leaving many exposed leg areas for Xavier to view and ponder. Xavier handed Michelle a cup, and while Michelle went to grab the cup, she could feel the warmth and visually observed the steam flowing from the liquid.

"Thank you," said Michelle. Michelle could feel the fireplace's warmth and began to soak up the moment while she and Xavier enjoyed the quiet of the room.

CHAPTER 5

"Michelle, do you mind if I ask what you do for a living and ask you some questions about you?" said Xavier.

Michelle pulled her hair back over her ear, took a small sip of her hot tea, and agreed to let Xavier into her personal life. "Well, I graduated from North New York State College and found a great career in the field of sex therapy," said Michelle.

"Wait, you have my full attention now, Michelle," said Xavier rather quickly. "What exactly does a sex therapist do?" asked Xavier.

Michelle could see Xavier was eager to learn her role as a therapist and said, "First, I assist people with ways to enhance their relationship objectives through discussion or exercising sexual scripts," said Michelle. "I also utilize ways of helping people discover sexual fantasies in a safe ambiance while identifying things that can trigger dangerous sexual triggers and ways to approach sex positively," explained Michelle. "Couples learn a lot about their selves and in return can apply what they have learned from their partner to enhance sexual pleasure and connection," said Michelle.

"I have to ask," said Xavier. "Does any of your patients ever get turned on to you from the interactions?" asked Xavier.

"Yes," explained Michelle. "Professionalism is the first step when working with people, and attraction is expected when exploring sexual conversations, but the practice of control is a high priority and never to be overstepped," explained Michelle.

Xavier became pleased with how professional and intelligent Michelle appeared as she brilliantly described her profession. Xavier studied Michelle's features and enjoyed how she adjusted her glasses when she talked and how she would sit with great posture while utilizing eye contact. Her hair and her lips' movement mixed with her voice's gentleness became a soothing factor for Xavier. As he listened to how professional and essential her job duties became, he was opened to a whole new world of how people need help in many ways. Xavier became increasingly curious and asked Michelle if she felt comfortable sharing some of her experiences. Michelle agreed and explained her profession includes many sexual occurrences and mature descriptions.

Xavier became more intrigued and said, "Please continue. I'm fascinated and eager to hear your interactions."

Michelle agreed and explained how a couple has been seeing her for several years due to a sexual practice that involved a deep underground experience that was unhealthy and illegal. Michelle explained, "People have a need to explore their sexuality and will go to great extremes to fulfill their need for lust even if it comes at the expense of their relationships." Michelle asked Xavier if he has heard of a sexual partner that swinger refer to as a "bull."

Xavier looked puzzled and said, "A bull, I would have to say, I immediately think of a bull from a pasture, but pretty sure it's going to be a guy."

Michelle cleared her throat, adjusted her glasses, and was eager to explain to Xavier what a bull was when referring to sexual partners. "A bull is a man that is driven to fuck," said Michelle. She continued to explain, "A bull is a guy who is generally large in appearance with striking features and fit while possessing a large penis and big hanging balls."

Xavier almost spat up his tea and laughed. "I'm sorry, this is interesting and unheard of on my end until now," explained Xavier.

Michelle pulled her hair back and positioned her body directly in front of Xavier and said, "Stay with me, and if it becomes too much, I will gladly stop."

Xavier placed his hand on Michelle's hand and said, "Please continue. Are you kidding?"

Michelle continued to explain how a bull usually holds no attachment or verbal communication when interacting with a lover.

"Wait, how is that possible?" asked Xavier.

Michelle responded, "A bull is a person who you take your lover to, and he will perform sexual acts in a private location while the other person watches."

Xavier's eyes became wide, and his mouth fell wide open and asked, "So you have a story that explains this practice in detail?"

Michelle looked at Xavier and responded, "Indeed, just as I explained earlier, I have a couple that has engaged in this type of interaction for many years and now experiences hardships within their marriage."

"I remember when the couple first came to me and started to explain how their high-profile marriage has declined and how they cannot agree on how to proceed forward with their sexual interactions as a couple," stated Michelle.

She explained how the husband and wife became interested in exploring sex within a deeper and more erotic setting. The husband and wife had reached a sexual high within their marriage that involved almost any type of sexual action you could imagine. The couple began watching several pornographic movies that involved dominance, submission, and exploring extreme sex acts. Eventually, their lust for sexual exploration began to be tempted by the need to explore these fantasies outside their bedroom setting. The husband and wife visited a private club where people would wear masks covering their faces while hiding their identities. Later that night, after meeting several couples, they were invited to go upstairs and become more intimate. The couple started by watching other couples fuck and then as they began to fuck found themselves desiring to be touched by other people. It became sexually stimulating on another level to be giving your husband head while another couple moaned and fucked within the same room. Michelle continued to explain how the wife told her about an interaction that involved her riding her husband and then another couple approaching them and asked if they could watch while next to them at proximity.

"This is the point where couples make a mistake and allow others to infiltrate their connection and bond," explained Michelle.

She explained how the wife and husband were utterly nude while experimenting with Molly, enhancing their sexual interactions. The wife was riding her husband while enjoying the fact that many couples could be visually observed in various positions fucking and moaning and exploring sexual interactions they had not tried. The couple that sat next to them started with the husband sitting facing her and his wife on her knees, sucking his dick aggressively. The couple's sight engaging in oral sex made the wife more aroused while she began to fuck her husband harder and faster. The couple's husband also agreed his sexual drive increased hundredfold by watching the woman perform oral sex while his wife rode his hard cock. The mistake happened when the wife was riding the husband and lost control of her balance and placed her hand on the woman's shoulder. Immediately, the other couple's wife caressed the wife's hand and pulled it down onto her breast while she continued to perform oral sex. The wife became endured with deep desires of sexual interactions. As she continued to ride her husband, she became enticed with the feeling of another woman's body and burned with intensified passion. Her husband enjoyed watching her caress another woman's breast and began to ejaculate within his wife's pussy when suddenly, the other woman rose and began to touch the wife and French kiss her deeply.

The woman who was sucking her mate was now interlocked with the husband's wife as he finished exploding his load within her pussy. The wife slid off the husband and continued to make out with the woman as the other woman found her way to her pussy and pulled open her legs and began to lick her cum-soaked vagina.

"The interaction was new and was something the wife has fantasied about for a while considering sex with a woman," explained Michelle.

The wife discovered how erotic it was watching and feeling another woman eat her husband's ejaculate from her willing pussy.

The wife told her the experience sent her into the most profound orgasm she has ever faced, and instead of being pleased, she was over-ridden with a desire for more. The wife continued to explain how she enjoyed her husband's desire to watch, and the sight of another man masturbating at the sight of her body drove her insane. As she screamed and pulses of pleasure electrified her body, she touched her husband and asked if she could finish the other man. The husband said he was reluctant at first and feeling a little confused, but at that moment, the other woman positioned herself and her extreme beauty and gently ran her hands down to his cock and said, "It's okay, just enjoy." She went down on her husband, and he began to moan and enjoy her talented mouth while the wife dropped to her knees and took the length of the other man deep into her mouth.

The wife explained how erotic and right the moment felt as desire and the feeling of being bad rushed through her body. She explained how her pussy was dripping from the excitement and found a deep passion to experience the taste of another man's cum exciting. She sucked hard up and down his shaft while continually finding her way to his balls and making popping sounds as she sucked them into her mouth. She felt so warm and flushed as he pulled her hair and rubbed her shoulders and breast. She said it became very intense as her husband began to cum into the woman's mouth and watched as she twisted her tongue around his head and continued in a slower motion up and down while swallowing his load. At that time, she said, she felt a sharp pull of her hair and the man's dick sinking deep in her throat as he unleashed his load all over her tongue and deep into her throat. She barely could contain the size of the load and gagged a little until she swallowed most of the warm sperm. The man shook while she enjoyed his taste and made sure to pump every drop from his nice cock into her belly. She said she loved how her husband guided the women's head up and down his dick while watching her swallow her man. After the experience, the couple explained how the interaction became a new line of sexual exploration and continued several times over the next year.

The two couple's interactions became an interaction regularly. The wife once explained to Michelle how they became fond of the couple they met at the private club and began to explore sexual inter-actions on a profound level. The couples would ride together late at night after dinner and drinks while the women would change part-ners. The husband would drive, and the other woman would ride in the front seat while the other wife would be in the back seat with the other man. The wife explained how exciting it was for her to take her shirt off and give the other man a blow job while riding in the back seat as her husband drove. The husband would admit the other wife would drop her head down in his lap as he drove and suck his dick as well while the wife took in her husband's length in the back seat. She explained how erotic it was to look up and see her husband trying to drive while getting his dick sucked and watching her head bob up and down through the rearview mirror while on another man in the back seat. She continued to explain how addicting the moment and taste of his cum became a driving factor to both the husband and the wife while the women pleased their hard dicks. The wife said it was exciting to see the other woman lift her head and wipe the excess cum from her lips and she finished swallowing her lover's load.

The blow jobs eventually lead to other's partners and other peo-ple within the club that hid their identities. The wife said they all were out on a date one night, and after several drinks, the other man placed his hand on her leg under the table and found his way pri-vately into her pussy. She described how discretely he fingered her pussy while they all talked and how difficult it was for her to con-trol her passion as she became wetter and pushed his fingers deeper into her body. The partners had shared each other orally but have refrained from fucking. The wife knew she should be consulting her husband first but enjoyed the presence of his fingers within her body. The wife said she asked her husband to walk her to the bathroom as she pulled the other man's fingers out of her wet pussy. The husband agreed, and while walking, the wife turned to him, pulled him into a more private area, and asked him straight out if he would let her fuck the other man. He immediately said yes and asked if it were okay if he could fuck the wife as well. The husband and wife became turned on beyond measure as the husband pulled the wife into the men's room, pulled up her short dress from the back, and fucked her hard against the stall wall while pulling out his dick and shooting his load onto her tight ass. Michelle continued to explain how the couple's interactions were now full force into sharing each other's partners and continued for a great time, leaving the door open for more intense interactions.

Michelle fanned her face as if she were hot and said, "In order to explain how people arrive at a different location within their lives, you have to be clear on their story."

Xavier laughed and said, "I get it. That is an intense story, and I want more."

Michelle started to visually detect that Xavier was becoming excited and overwhelmed with curiosity. She found the interaction stimulating and fun. The exchange was the first time within a date she has shared a story and has found it to be highly erotic while laughing and being free to be silly. Michelle paused after laughing with Xavier, and both were detecting a heightened sense of erotic arousal from the exploration of the story.

"Okay, let's continue, or do you need a pause so you can get some sleep?" asked Michelle.

"You know, let's keep going. I'm going to drop my appointment for tomorrow because I'm having a wonderful time."

Michelle was pleased with Xavier's willingness to continue the night.

"Do you need another beer or some more hot tea?" asked Xavier.

"I'm good, thank you," responded Michelle while leaning forward and touching his hand slightly.

Xavier laughed sort of loudly and said, "I'm going to be truthful and relieved because, as a man, I have had an adverse reaction to your story and a little embarrassed."

Michelle responded, "As a sex therapist."

The moment stopped as they exploded into laughter and continued to laugh for several seconds and agreed they both understood how the moment could lead to things "popping up," said Michelle.

Xavier was about to lost it and he said, "Okay, let's continue this interesting explanation of a bull that I'm feverously waiting to hear."

CHAPTER 6

"What drives a person is a person's need for desire and curiosity," explained Michelle. She continued to explain how people find a good place within their lives, and as humans, we keep desiring more and more when sometimes the more was not what we expected.

"I'm not sure if I'm following you, Michelle," explained Xavier.

Michelle continued to explain how the couple she was counseling would provide significant information within the exchange that provided a snapshot of their lives leading up to the problems. The couple had a great marriage, but once they wanted more, they allowed desire to overtake their commitment to one another and allowed for other people to become part of their sexual relationship slowly.

"Oh, it's like adding another flavor to your favorite ice cream and discovering how something different can be tasty as well and pleasing to the senses," explained Xavier.

"Not saying there is anything wrong with adding a flavor to your favorite ice cream, but the analogy helps us understand that some things are better left for fantasy and imagination than exploring," said Michelle.

"Yep, the old saying, you can't have the cake and ice cream all the time," expressed Xavier.

Michelle continued to describe how the couple continued to explore their sexuality. Several times after their first encounter with the first couple, they included exciting things, such as flying out of town and tempting a waiter while they were out for dinner. Michelle explained, "The wife once was dared by the husband to flirt with the waiter and challenged to see if she could give him oral sex."

She continued to describe how the wife would touch the waiter's hand or how she purposely unbuttoned her shirt, exposing a significant amount of breast for him to observe. She noticed the younger waiter was stuttering and becoming fidgety and went for it. She asked him to come close and whispered in his ear that she wanted to give him a blow job. The waiter looked confused and looked back at the husband while the wife grabbed his arm and said it's okay with him.

The waiter looked back at her and said, "Okay, I finish my shift in twenty minutes."

The wife looked at him and said, "No, now in the men's bathroom."

He looked around and then indicated for her to follow him. He went into the bathroom, came back, opened the door, led her to the rear stall, and shut the door. The wife immediately pulled her shirt off and exposed her big breast and hit her knees and looked up to him while he unzipped his pants and hung his long meat out for her enjoyment. The wife said that these kinds of challenges became addicting, and she would burn with desire from the memories of random men using her mouth and exploding on her breasts.

The more she and her husband played, the more challenges eventually jumped to his side, and she asked him to fuck a random woman in their car. She said it was exciting watching their naked bodies through the window and his ass forcefully going in and out in motion while he rammed his load deep inside another woman's pussy in the spot where she would sit. She liked watching the woman wrap her legs around her husband's back and noticed how she would grip his hips when he was hitting the right spot. She said she enjoyed watching her husband suck a woman's breasts as well as slipping his tongue deep into her mouth. Another time, the wife described how her husband asked one of his close friends to let his wife suck his dick; of course, the friend said yes and participated eagerly.

The husband explained how he drove his wife and friend around at night while they were in the back seat and observed their interactions through the car's rearview mirror. He enjoyed watching her head bounce up and down while her mouth was sunk deep on his penis and loved watching the friend's reactions as he came into his wife's mouth and tried to contain the feelings of pleasure screaming out. Soon, the more minor interactions of sex turned into double penetration and multiple lovers within the same bedding. He described how he and his wife began to want more intense taboo interactions and began fucking multiple people every weekend. Their desire for each other's bodies had transformed to a desire to fuck many people and often resulting in them never touching each other throughout an entire weekend.

"Wow, you see these kinds of things on TV, but to hear it in real life is crazy," explained Xavier.

"Yes, their desire for another has morphed into an all-out desire to see them fucking other people every week," said Michelle. "The couple had lost control and began down a forbidden road that is going to be hard to change direction," explained Michelle. She continued to present the following steps within the journey of the couple. The husband said he had become a little bored watching his wife suck someone's dick or him fucking a random woman in a car.

"Their interactions with others lead them deeper into an exploration of sexual drugs and experiences you would only think were created in movies," explained Michelle.

She explained how the husband was invited to a particular place with one of their sexual partners while his wife gave his wife oral sex in another room with other couples. The invitee explained how their wives would be busy for hours with the other couples and wanted to show him something secretive but stimulating without fear of people knowing what he was doing. The couple's husband was interested, agreed, and traveled a few minutes by car to a building outside a dock area. The companion explained to keep close to him and let him do the talking. As they approached a door and rang the bell, he provided his identity badge and introduced his visitor. The door buzzed, and they walked into a darkened hall with a stairway leading downward and lit by tiny lights at the steps.

The husband became intrigued by the environment by observing women on their knees giving oral sex in darkened corners and catching people fucking as they passed by the random room. The husband said he stopped and watched a woman spread out naked on a table while several men jacked off onto her body while she arched her back and played with her pussy. He started to understand why his friend brought him to this place and was intrigued by others' actions and the excitement of the people being dirty. His friend urged him to continue following and asked where he was taking him. The friend said he would show him something taboo and quite different from anything he had encountered. The husband became curious and wondered what he could be experiencing.

His friend spoke quietly to another person at the door. While the person asked several more questions of who he was, they both were ordered to take a stairway down several flights and into a room, leaving their clothing and personal items in lockers and standing naked in the line at the door. "Trust me, this is worth the requirements and mind-blowing," explained the friend.

As the door opened, they followed several other men and a couple of women into a room with elevated seats surrounding a wooden bench in the middle of the room. The room was surrounded by rock walls and rock flooring that felt wet as if water were sprayed across the floor while containing torches burning around the perimeter areas. A man dressed in full black leather instructed the people to sit in the chairs and went over some rules. He explained, "First, do not engage the interactions within the lit area. If you do, you will be removed and never to return." He continued to explain, "Second, have some fucking fun. Third, no one speaks to the bull or interacts with the bull, and if they do, the bull has the freedom to do as he fucking wants." The man became silent and said, "You are in his domain now, anything goes, and if he wants your ass, then he will take what he wants, no questions asked." The man screamed and said, "Now, get on your knees as we prepare for the bull."

The man laughed loudly and walked over to one of the women in the line of people who entered the room and spoke quietly to her and a person who appeared to be her mate. He took her by the hand as her mate kissed her mouth and walked her over to the wooden bench. He had her sit down on the floor with her ass on top of her calves and asked her to submit to the "bull fully." The husband explained he thought, *What the fuck is a bull?* He leaned over to his friend and asked him if he had brought him to some freaky bestiality entertainment and was not into that kind of sexuality.

"Hold on, you will see. I promise it will be worth the time," explained the friend.

Music began to play in the background, which appeared to be Nine Inch Nails' "Closer." The husband gazed eagerly, trying to understand what was about to unfold as he saw this beautiful woman sitting on her knees with her hands on her lap and her big breast positioned out for everyone's enjoyment. Two men appeared in the background dressed in full leather and pulling some rope while eventually revealing a large naked man wearing a bull's horns draped with brown leather down the back of his neck. As the figures came more into view, he noticed the men taking the rope off the large man and falling to the ground. The man with the horns leaned back and stretched open his arms up in the air and let out a loud roar.

What the fuck is this? thought the husband. He noticed the man was more than six feet in height and total muscle. He could not help but see his colossal dick semihard and hanging toward the right and was amazed at his hanging balls' size. *This man is massive and hung like a fucking bull,* thought the husband. The bull approached the woman and stood directly in front of her with his massive cock directly in front of her mouth. The husband noticed he was starting to become excited and looked around the room to observe men rubbing their cocks while the remaining woman was directly in front of her lover and starting to give him head while her bare ass exposed her pussy from behind. In front of the bull, the woman looked terrified but sexually stimulated at the man's mammoth size and his genitals.

The bull aggressively grabbed the woman's hair with his right hand and took his length into his left hand, telling her to "open your wet mouth and suck my big dick." The woman leaned forward while her big breast dangled before her and rubbed her hands up his muscular legs and finding their way to his six-packed shaped waist while opening her mouth wide and sucking one of his large balls into her mouth. The bull leaned his head back and let out a beastly roar as the woman clenched her eyes shut and rolled her tongue around his balls and eventually sliding her mouth onto his thick shaft.

The husband began to find himself stroking his cock while watching the woman struggle to stretch open her mouth, trying to take in his girth. He noticed the massive length of his dick as she had both hands wrapped around the shaft and still possessed room for her mouth to slide over his big cock head. The bull leaned forward while the husband noticed his darkened eye shadowing and what appeared to be handsomely orange contacts in color, adding to the image. The bull's arms were massively sculpted like a world-champion bodybuilder gripping now both sides of her blond-colored hair and forcefully shoving his dick deep into her throat area while she gagged with fluids running down her chin and dipping on her perfect breast.

He aggressively mouth fucked her while pulling her body back and forth like she weighed one pound. The husband noticed her eyes were watering while her mascara ran down her face, creating a stimulating image of intense oral sex. The husband saw the couple directly arouse from him, intensifying their oral sex interaction, and when he began to ejaculate into his mate's mouth, he let out a loud moan.

Immediately, the bull became enraged and pushed the woman who was sucking his dick to the side and yelled two inches from his face, "If you do not shut the fuck up, I will fuck your pretty whore in her tight little ass with my big dick."

The man looked terrified as his dick was still dripping cum and became limp quickly. The bull stood up and grabbed the man's mate by her back hips from behind and said, "I will sink every inch into her if I hear you again."

The man shook his head in terror while his mate sat quickly beside him.

CHAPTER 7

The husband began to understand this situation and became increasingly interested in the control and dynamics the event was providing. He understood how this was the filler he needed to satisfy his sexual needs and imagined his wife playing the bull's lover's role. The bull was terrifying beyond imagination and full of sexual rage that energized the entire room while men started to aggressively stroke their dicks faster. The bull walked quickly back to the submissive lover, pulled her up off the ground, and laid her on her back positioned on the wooden bench. He forcefully spread her legs as she gasped and held onto his horns as he buried his tongue deep into the folds of her wet pussy. The husband became more sexually intrigued and wanted nothing more than for his wife to be on that table as he observed the woman rolling her head back and forth while moaning out loud as the bull licked, sucked, and bit her pussy area.

After several minutes of devouring her pussy, he flipped her over the side of the table and started to mount her from behind. He placed one hand on her left hip and the other onto her right while pressing his bulging dick into the depths of her pussy. The woman caressed one of her breasts while letting out a scream of pleasure and pain as his long dick began sliding in and out of her wet pussy. The bull's fucking turned into violent waves of thrusting and deep penetration that aggressively shook the woman's body and left her pleading for him to cum in her pussy. The husband caught sight of how the bull's massive balls hang and swung back and forth, smacking the clit area of the woman's pussy and causing her to drip onto the table while driving her to roll her eyes in pleasure. Her breast nipples were hard, and her double-Ds swung back and forth while smacking sounds of flesh colliding filled the room. The woman screamed, moaned, and pleaded for his dick to fuck her any way he wanted. The bull placed both hands on her shoulders and would thrust his length violently into her pussy while leaving dark red areas on her shoulders where he was biting her flesh and causing blood to stream down her back.

The husband began to feel his balls tightening and let out a quiet grunt as his cum shot upward and covered his stomach and dick areas. He noticed many men coming at different times and observed how the woman across the room was fingering her pussy while watching the bull command his lover's pussy. The bull fucked with intensity, and while the woman continued to moan loudly and drip onto the table, the bull pulled his dick from her pussy that glistened with wetness in the light and began to roar again as he released his thick load onto the back area of the woman. The load was massive and splashed across her ass and entire back area while splattering her hair and dripping off her sides. The bull's muscles were highlighted by the shine of sweat and blood pumping through his veins as he slowed his release of cum onto the woman's back. He reached forward and pulled her hair aggressively, positioning her head in a backward position while sinking his exploding cock back into her throbbing pussy and sucking on her exposed neck. He slowly moved his dick in and out while spilling the remains of his load within her body and felt up her lovely, rounded breast. The bull pushed her forward onto the table while slipping out of her body and allowing his unhanded dick to collapse as strings of cum stretched from the tip of his cock toward the floor.

The bull stood silent as he gazed around the room; the husband looked amazed at how big and low his cock and balls were hanging and could easily see why the woman on the table had smeared eye mascara and wholly withdrawn from the moment by the intense fuck that just invaded her deep inside her body. She laid flat on her belly with her arms hanging down the sides of the table and her legs wide open while her pussy was red, swollen, and draining thick white cum onto the table. The bull's chest compressed with a fast rhythm of breathing and began to walk over to the man and woman he screamed at earlier for making noise. His massive silhouette stood in front of them as he gazed at the man's mate and grabbed her by the throat, pulling her into the air while she was struggling and gasping for air. The moment was intense and frightful while everyone was afraid to move, fearing the repercussions of their intentions. The woman's mate jumped up and grabbed the bull's arms and caused the bull to throw his woman across the room onto the hard floor, causing her to cry in pain. The bull grabbed the man with both hands and lifted him into the air, throwing him into the high-raised seating areas. The bull walked over the woman he threw, pulled her over his shoulders, and walked out the doorway in the back he entered through while the two men who escorted him in stood guard after they secured the door.

The husband explained to Michelle how exciting the events and left him longing to invite his wife. A door opened across the room, revealing a lighted path when a man walked in and asked the crowd to exit this way. The husband explained how he told his friend how the event was crazy intense and loved the acting. As they walked out, the man who had the mate taken from him was screaming and pleading with the guards to return her. The husband was amazed at the interactions and the quality of the acting, and how he was left wanting more. The husband and his friend were directed back to the locker areas where they were instructed to get dressed.

"That was fucking great, man. I want to know how I can have my wife meet the bull," said the husband to his friend.

The friend looked at him and said, "Are you sure?"

The husband continued to explain how his desire was overflowing from the need to see his wife take the bull and to capture the image of her face as he slid his length into her vagina as he looked with pleasure. The men continued out of the dressing area and into a dimly lit large room filled with many people and a bar area. As they walked through, the visual sex actions continued; he noticed a woman on her knees under a table serving up a blow job on a man leaned back with a cigar in one hand and his hand placed on her dark hair, gliding her up and down. Another scene involved a woman riding a man in a chair with his hands cupping her ass checks and deeply embraced while kissing.

As they passed through, they were instructed to keep right to exit or left for pleasure. Already intoxicated by the evening entertainment, they decided to explore a little deeper. The two men found an open room with two men on a bed while engaged in a sexual act that involved the man fucking his ass slowly while the other man gripped the sheets tightly. He noticed women engaging in oral sex with other women and men swapping from woman to woman in an open format that involved a free-for-all fuck. The husband was intrigued with actions within the room and had engaged with similar activities but not on this level or within this type of darkened environment. The husband explained how he had become curious while watching the two men engage in sex and started to become aroused as he found his way to a bench and observed the interactions. He explained how he loved a woman's feel but always wondered what a man would feel like intertwined within a sexual moment.

As he and his friend sat and watched, he asked his friend, "Have you ever fucked a man?"

His friend replied, "I have a couple of times and liked the excitement."

The husband became more intrigued and found his gaze watching the two men fuck and how the man's dick flopped back and forth while partly hard as his ass was invaded by a hard cock. The husband's friend placed his hand on his leg and began to rub lightly. The husband explained he was overridden by desire and moved his friend's hand onto his genital area. The friend stood up, pulled his shirt off, and unbuckled his belt, allowing his pants to fall to the floor, exposing his nakedness while positioning his body on his knees directly in front of the husband. The husband did not resist the offer and unzipped his pants, pulling out his quickly hardening dick and allowing his friend to take his stiff dick within his soft, warm mouth. The husband gasped from the hard sucking pressure the friend applied as he overlooked the two men fucking in the center of the room. The interaction was different and compelling while he engaged in oral sex with a man.

As his friend sucked him hard, another man walked across the room and leaned over to his friend and whispered in his ear. The new member grabbed his bulging cock, dropped droplets of lube onto his ass, and started pushing his dick into his friend's ass. The husband described how intense the sucking action became as he felt his friend moaning in pleasure and pain as the other man fucked him in the ass. The fucking lasted several minutes as he began to feel his balls tightening and his cum preparing to flow into his friend's mouth. He leaned back and shot his load into his mouth as he drained every drop. The other man started to slow his movement and began to moan as he exploded into his friend's ass while jerking and pulsing from the ejaculation.

The husband said he enjoyed the different stimulation and took in the moment as his friend moaned with pleasure and finished his leaking dick as the other man dumped his load into his body. The husband noticed his friend had been jerking off and came all over the floor as they both finished. As they both dressed and sat for an awkward moment, the husband asked if they could leave. They agreed to go, and as they walked down a long hall passing many doors, they decided they needed to find their way back to their wives. As they approached a doorway, a man handed them a card with info and said to schedule another visit when they were ready but keep in mind that this was a private club and needed to be discreet. The door opened, and they found their way to their car, where they sat silent.

The man asked the husband, "Did I go too far?"

The husband replied, "No, I did what I wanted and do not regret the moment." He continued to explain he thought his wife would be well-pleased to hear he engaged with another man but was unsure if he would want to repeat the occurrence because he liked women.

"I fell into the moment and tried something different than I had fantasized and hope it doesn't make things weird between us?" asked the husband.

"No, all cool, it was the heat of the moment, and it felt good," explained the friend.

CHAPTER 8

Xavier's mouth hung wide open, and he could feel his sexual energy about to burst out of his body. Michelle smiled and felt much excitement and wondered if she shared a little too much of her interactions with other people's lives. Michelle explained how she was worried about the couple's experimentation and the path the couple has chosen and fearing the newly sexual course would destroy their relationship.

"I'm really at a loss of words and shocked at things people do and what is available within our societies," said Xavier.

Michelle agreed and explained, "People are the same. We all just approach stages in our lives much differently."

Michelle continued to explain how people judge one another. Still, for some, they partake in drug use, some use alcohol to cover up troubles, others engage in sexual affairs, porn, or even commit crimes to help control things within their lives.

"We all have that one thing we do differently and tell ourselves because mine is different, it's not as bad as theirs when in fact it's the same," explained Michelle.

Xavier nodded and said, "That makes sense of why people are the way they are and why they choose different triggers within their lives."

Xavier asked Michelle if she would like to hear a story from his profession but was unsure if he could match what he just overheard.

"Absolutely," eagerly stated Michelle as she turned her body a little more toward Xavier and setting down her finished tea.

Xavier quickly gazed discreetly as Michelle adjusted her position in front of him. As she turned, he could see the inner portions of her smooth, shiny legs and started to find his mind wondering as to what lies beneath her covered areas.

"Xavier," asked Michelle.

"Sorry, I became lost for a moment," explained Xavier.

Michelle was pleased as she caught Xavier adoring her tanned legs and found the peeking exciting. Xavier asked if Michelle would excuse him for a moment as he made his way to his bathroom. Xavier entered his bathroom and stood in front of his mirror with both hands on each side and stared at himself while pondering if he should make a move and embrace Michelle. Xavier said to himself, "She is beautiful and perfect. I do not want to mess this up, for I have never felt such a strong connection to a woman." Xavier's mind keeps going back to the feel of her body next to his and the image of his glance at her large breast and the perfect ass he caught sight of within his mirror. He felt his dick stiffening with rushes of blood and very much wanted to be inside of Michelle's body. Xavier regained his thoughts as he stood for a time, trying to control his intentions and desires.

Meanwhile, while sitting on the sofa, Michelle pondered the same thoughts and was amazed Xavier had not tried to pursue her body. Michelle was comfortable with Xavier and wanted badly to take all her clothes off and offer her body in a nude state for his pleasure once he returned. "What the fuck, Michelle, get a grip and try not to mess this up," spoke Michelle quietly. The moment and Xavier were different for her, and even though she wanted to lay with him, she also felt a desire to be proper and respectful of how he has refrained from touching her when faced with her extreme advances. Michelle pulled her legs close to her chest and wrapped her arms around her knees and imagined how she never wanted this night to end as she felt the warmth of the fire and soaked in the presence of Xavier.

Xavier returned and sat gently in front of Michelle and said he wanted to share a story from his journalism adventures. "My adventures are probably not as interesting as yours, but I do have some eventful encounters I can share," said Xavier. Xavier continued to draw Michelle's attention and curiosity as he began to share a story he was working on currently that involved local disappearances of several people.

Xavier explained how several people have become missing within a hundred-mile radius of their city over the past few years. "I believe these disappearances are connected, and I'm going to keep exploring until I can find a connection."

Michelle gasped and said, "I have heard so much information concerning the disappearances and have become a little paranoid myself when going out." Michelle asked, "Does the police have any leads?"

Xavier took a deep breath and sadly admitted, "No, the police have shared minor findings and have expressed how the case is becoming more difficult to establish clues and persons on interest."

Xavier explained how several women and a couple of men have become missing while police have reported finding bodies in random proximity areas. One woman was found naked, lying in the woods with her body spread out like a jumping jack position while a clean circle was formed around her body with candles. The woman's body was discovered by a person hunting on some local land, noticed the sight of glowing candles, and became curious about the light source and terrified at what he had discovered.

Michelle covered her mouth with her hand and said, "The news has not released this kind of information. Do you think this is the work of a serial killer?"

Xavier asked Michelle to please keep what he was saying between them and stressed that it could cause problems for the ongoing investigations if the information were released. Xavier continued to explain how his sources had shared information concerning the bodies that seem to be connected to some pattern. In contrast, the bodies displayed severe bruising, cuts, and markings while being sexually violated.

"I believe the murders are part of a more significant operation, and while I cannot share all my information, I believe there are many agents involved," explained Xavier. "Two more bodies were reported to have been found in an abandoned church positioned in a vicarious position," said Xavier.

Xavier continued to explain how a man's body was strung up by rope with one hand positioned toward the ground. At the same time, another woman was nude, placed in a submission position at the person's feet, and surrounded by candles once again. Both bodies were sexually violated, with extreme bruising and cut.

"I need access to the crime scene photos so I can try to establish a connection, motive, and if there is a pattern," explained Xavier.

Xavier continued to explain how the murders seem to be connected because of the pentagram and candle similarities.

"I'm creeped out right now," said Michelle. "I sit here and think about how I have been too comfortable when allowing myself to interact with people, especially when on a date," explained Michelle.

Xavier looked at Michelle and expressed a sense of urgency, hoping she felt comfortable with him. Michelle once again pulled her hair back with her fingers and urged Xavier that she felt safe and happy to be here with him.

"Okay, enough with this stressful dialogue of your profession. Do you want to hear more about the couple I have been counseling?" asked Michelle.

"I'm sorry, I know what I do for a living can be negative, and I would enjoy hearing more about your couple," explained Xavier.

"Okay, are you sure my forwardness and the adult content is okay?" asked Michelle.

"Absolutely," expressed Xavier.

Michelle began to pick up where she left off concerning how the couple went from sexually explorative to all-out sharing partners and engaging in taboo sexual parties. "The wife came to me and wanted to speak about the club and interactions she discovered from her husband," said Michelle. She explained how the wife was shocked and confused when she learned how he let their friend suck his cock while being fucked in the ass.

Michelle said the wife did explain how she stayed back at the private club with the other wife and did engage in sexual acts while drinking heavily, but her husband was always present and left without consulting her. She continued to explain how she was lost in the moment while engaging in profound sexual acts with the other wife and became attracted to her body and how she touched her. The couple had always engaged in sexual acts together with an agreement of taking care of each other. Still, the wife felt the husband violated their agreement and had found something he preferred much better than their encounters together. She explained how the moment was different when going down on another woman or man when her husband was present and how they both were in this together while feeling the encounters were part of their sexual journey and part of how they pleased each other.

"I explained how she needs to open up and bring this concern up to her husband and emphasize how she feels a separation when he does not participate with her while venturing out on his own," explained Michelle.

"I think I understand where she is coming from, not saying I have participated in those types of actions, but I think she feels the sex with others is an extension of their sexual moment as long as they are together," explained Xavier.

Michelle said the wife continued to explain how her husband has started to go out with just the other man while leaving the two women together at home or encouraging them to go out together without them. She explained how the wife could not understand why he had pushed them aside, especially when the other wife was superhot and willing to do anything he liked. When the couples share, her husband could fuck the other woman's mouth, ass, or pussy without restrictions. Michelle explained how she asked the wife if she thinks the husband had become bored of their routine encounters as a couple duo and possibly searching for something new or different. The wife agreed with Michelle's thought and began to think he was pulling apart from their sexual connection and searching for a new clique that brings a different kind of excitement.

"I explained the only way to know for certain was to ask if you can go out with them and become part of this new adventure," said Michelle. "So I encouraged her to see what all the excitement was and maybe she could entice her husband or discover what he is searching for in that establishment."

The wife agreed and told Michelle that she would ask her husband to let her go with them to the private establishment and was willing to be open to what he was searching for and what his needs had become. The wife did admit the story he shared concerning the bull was interesting and would like to explore the entertainment firsthand.

CHAPTER 9

Xavier looked at Michelle with great curiosity and asked, "Well, did she go with her husband?"

Michelle said the session had ended on that point and has not met with the couple since their last meeting.

"Are you serious?" asked Xavier.

Michelle looked at Xavier and laughed and said, "Sorry, I wish I had more concerning the husband and wife, but I'm sure she will be able to share more interesting details as their exploration unfolds."

Xavier quickly responded and said, "I'm looking forward to hearing the continuation of the interactions."

Michelle placed her cup on the table and said, "It's getting very late, and I have lost track of time while overstaying my welcome."

Xavier placed his hand on her shoulder and asked her to please stay the night. Michelle felt a deep tickle within her pussy as the excitement of him asking her to stay was pleasing to her ears.

"I would love to stay the night if it's not too much trouble," expressed Michelle.

"No trouble at all. You can have my room, and I will sleep here on this comfy couch," said Xavier.

"I hate to take your room," said Michelle.

"It would be my pleasure for you to stay. Come with me, and I will help you settle in," said Xavier.

He showed her where more blankets were if she needed more and begged her to please ask him if she needed anything at all. Michelle wondered if he may be hinting to her, asking him to join her in his bed but held back the urge to become that forward.

"I'm glad you're staying with me, have a good night's sleep. I'll be just outside the door if you need me," expressed Xavier.

The door closed, and Michelle sat on the side of the bed, taking in the evening's wonderful feeling and how alive she felt. Michelle stood up from knowing she could not possibly sleep from the onset of sexual frustration and began to sneak around the room with curiosity. She found herself back at his dresser and picked up his cologne and breathed in the odor while revealing it was Eternity by Calvin Klein. The smell sent pleasing sensations throughout her body as she found herself rubbing the side of her neck and thinking of how pleasant it was smelling the cologne on his body earlier that evening. Michelle continued to snoop around and found it exciting while finding the small things of Xavier's life laid out before her. She picked up one of his opt eds and began to read the story of how he investigated a small town near them that was experiencing a string of localized theft and became lost with the way he described events and how he flowed his words. She read through the article and discovered writing on the back, revealing how the piece was his first published investigation and included a small note from his parents of how proud they were of his accomplishments. She continued to look around, and after several minutes, she wanted to get a cup of water for her bedside. Michelle walked up to the door quietly and placed her ear next to the wood and felt Xavier was probably asleep and proceeded to open the door quietly while tiptoeing her way to the kitchen.

Michelle proceeded quietly and found her way to the sink. As she looked up, she could see the sofa facing her direction, and to her amazement, she found Xavier laying on the couch with his shirt off and his cock in his hand, stroking it slowly. She quickly ducked and thought, *Oh my, should I make a noise, or should I just walk over and ask him if I can take care of his hard state?* Out of curiosity, she slowly raised her head and watched him pull his hand up and down his dick. Xavier moved his head toward her direction, and she quickly ducked once again, but she found herself wanting to watch and proceeded to be sneaky once again and peeked over the counter. As Michelle's eyes caught sight of Xavier's body, she could not help but become sexually burning with desire as she watched his hand beat his hardened meat while his balls would move up and down ever so often. She admired his chest muscles as they tightened and wondered if he thought about her as he worked his load to the surface. Michelle did not care now if he caught her gaze and become stimulated at the sight of his body masturbating before her. She felt her pussy tingling from the excitement and her face becoming flushed with warmth as he began to moan quietly.

Michelle watched with much excitement and found her imagination acting out a scene of her naked breast over his body while she pleased him with her wet mouth. She watched as his motions became faster and his chest started to rise upward as he let out a tiny breath of pleasure while his dick spurted a wave of cum upward and splashing on his chest area. *I want to lick every drop of his load off his belly area,* thought Michelle as she watched with great effort. His mouth was wide open as his head leaned back with pleasure as his dick pumped waves of cum out onto his body. Michelle had seen many cocks cum while pulling out of her pussy or jerking on her breast but never witnessed a man in private playing with his hard dick. The excitement of the moment and the secretive state appealed to Michelle as she watched him slow his motions while his dick emptied the remaining stored sperm.

She licked her lips and pushed her fingers into her swollen pussy as she watched his cum roll down the back of his hand and down over his balls. When he finished, she could visually observe his heightened breathing patterns by how his chest pushed quickly up and down while his hand laid on his belly within the fresh presence of cum. By this point, Michelle was visually mesmerized and thoroughly rubbing her clit with a fast pace, trying to take in the moment and achieve an orgasm.

Michelle began to feel her body tightening as she tried to control the sound of her wet pussy popping from her vigorous rubbing action as she caught sight of Xavier moving to sit up from his sexual moment. She ducked quickly while pulling her fingers from her warm pussy and seeing a significant amount of clear ooze on her fingers. She became nervous and scanned the room while holding up her wet fingers in fear of her juices dripping onto the floor. Michelle felt a surge of startle as she heard Xavier walking. Not knowing what to do, she slid quickly under the table and held her position tightly. Xavier, within seconds, walked into the kitchen and stood just in front of the table where Michelle was hiding. Michelle could not help but notice the light highlighting his load and observed his semihard dick hanging over his balls as it appeared he was wiping excess cum from the tip and removing the amount from his belly area. Michelle was like a cat frozen just before pouncing on its prey and took extreme caution not to give up her position. It appeared Xavier filled a glass with water and then turned her direction and leaned against the counter with his dick hanging within feet from her face. She found his shape and hanging ball sack while wanting to slip out and suck his length into her mouth. Xavier then turned and proceeded back to the sofa as Michelle slowly made her way back to her room and laid on his bed.

Michelle's heart pounded from the onset of observing Xavier jacking off on his sofa while saying in her mind, *Damn, Michelle, that was too fucking close, and what were you thinking?* Michelle lay there with her eyes closed and replayed the vision over in her mind while her hands began to find their way down his shorts she had been wearing. Michelle sat up and pulled off all her clothing, revealing her body within a nude state on Xavier's bed, and began to rub her breasts while sliding her finger up and down her erect clit. She could only think about how good his hard cock would have felt in her mouth and deep in her pussy while steadily increasing her finger speeds within her vagina. Michelle's pussy was full of creamy cum and popped loudly as she vigorously stroked her wetness. Pulling her hand from her pussy quickly, she heard a noise and jumped up and turned Xavier's radio on low to cover the sounds of her masturbating within his bed. Michelle walked back to the bed, placed her left hand on the sheets while sticking her ass out toward the wall, and spread her nicely cut legs open. Michelle could see how her pussy cum stretched between her wet fingers and became tempted to place them in her mouth, tasting her juices.

She sucked the clear watery fluids from her fingers while she closed her eyes and found the taste of her pussy pleasing while pushing her vagina open and began jacking off with intensity. Michelle's breasts hang beautifully with hard nipples as she began to bury her face deep in Xavier's sheets, letting out an intense scream from the onset of her orgasm that started to drip down on the hardwood floor. Her body became flushed with warmth and began to pulse and jerk in waves as her pussy spurted out clear liquids onto his bed. Michelle fell forward as she finished lightly, rubbing her convulsing pussy and continued to moan deep into his bedding with a release unlike she has ever felt. As Michelle finished, she noticed she had squirted all over his bedding and well onto the flooring.

What just happened? asked Michelle within her mind. She observed her juices everywhere from the sheets, hardwood, and utterly soaked pussy running down her legs. She ran into the bathroom and quietly rewashed her body while continuously thinking about how badly she wanted to fuck Xavier. Michelle spent much time during that night cleaning up her sexual bliss from his room and eventually covered up with his bedding and comfortably fell soundly asleep.

CHAPTER 10

The following day, Michelle woke to a knock on her door while in Xavier's bed, and while covering her naked body, she said, "Come in."

Xavier walked in and sat on the side of the bedding and said, "I had the best evening last night and wanted to ask if I could see you again or leave you my contact number?"

Michelle pulled the covers up against her neck and sat up, saying, "I would love to see you again, and thank you for a wonderful evening."

Xavier quickly explained how he was sorry to awaken her so early. Still, he had to head out and meet with local resources concerning finding another body and hoping he could receive more information concerning the murders. "I am sorry, one of my resources said they have vital information concerning another murder, and I must leave at once. I have left you money for a cab, and I must see you again," said Xavier.

Xavier sat quietly for a moment and then leaned over Michelle and softly kissed her cheek and told her she was stunning and looked nice laying in his bed with a crooked smile.

Michelle blushed and said, "You are one of the sweetest people I have met, and can we meet at my place tomorrow night for dinner at seven?"

Xavier was delighted to hear Michelle asked him out again on another date and gladly accepted the invention.

"I will leave my information and address on your kitchen table," explained Michelle.

Xavier proceeded to leave the room, stopped, and turned his head, looked at Michelle with a smile once again and said, "Stay as long as you like and use anything you want."

Michelle waved bye and inside uttered, "What I want is hanging between your legs."

Michelle proceeded to get dressed as Xavier left for the day. She called a local cab, and while riding in the back seat, she could not stop thinking about the local murders and what if this guy driving all of a sudden locked the doors and proceeded off into the country with her captive. Michelle tried to clear her paranoid mind and replayed several events that unfolded throughout the night in her mind that made her happy. She considered how she loved to date men and experience how they all make love differently, but her mind kept going back to how Xavier treated her and how the evening made her feel like a woman and not just a date. Michelle continued to think about how she will give this a try, and when she said try, she will consider the thought of one man and one lover if this worked out. She was no stranger to men and their cocks and loved to be taken advantage of while displaying her unique talents within the bedroom, but something was different with Xavier, and her instincts told her he was different and unique.

Michelle arrived at her apartment and exited the cab while leaving a nice tip supplied by Xavier. She was impressed how he took care of her throughout the night and into the next day, assuring her a safe return to her home. Any other man would have fucked her ass off and then left it at that while reaching back out only to fuck again. She was good with that and had lived this type of life for several years while becoming fond of a man's dick within her body on regular occasions with no strings attached.

After walking into her apartment and sitting in a chair within her room, Michelle grabbed her diary next to her bedding and began to explore her life throughout the years. Michelle needed to investigate this strange feeling toward Xavier; was this for real, or was this a kind of sexual fascination from the onset of him denying sexual contact? She opened her diary and went back a few years; she reflected where she met a guy at a local bar who was charming, and after a few drinks, he asked her to go back to his place. The two of them arrived at his house and walked up the stairs while entering the home. He asked Michelle if he could take her to his bedroom. Michelle agreed, and they proceeded down to the basement, which was dark with very little light and a slightly cool feeling. She continued to read how they embraced deep, wet kissing and began to explore each other's bodies with their hands. The man pulled Michelle slightly onto the bed, and with surprise, she felt the bedding move like water and found the bedding to be a waterbed. Her date continued to guide her willing body down onto the softness of the bedding. Michelle could recall the comfort of the waterbed as they began to embrace in deeper kissing and touching.

Michelle felt the warmth of his hand slid down the front of her pants, finding its way to her pussy. Her diary revealed how warm his fingers felt as they began to penetrate her pussy folds and rub her clit. His hand, caressing her wet pussy clit, sent pulses of desire through her body while their tongues found their way into each other's mouth. She read how she began to respond to the sensations and placed her hand on the outside of his pants and began to massage his hardening cock through his clothing. Michelle unbuttoned her pants, allowing her zipper to supply more area for his hand to pleasure her vagina. Her date pulled out his long cock and placed her soft hand on the shaft as Michelle began to stroke his dick up and down.

The darkened room and the waterbed mixed with sexual stimulation were pleasing to Michelle, leading to deeper stimulation of their private parts and their clothing wholly removed. She could recall the feeling of how he sucked her neck while leading down to her erect nipples and how he commented the liking of how big her breast appeared. His tongue was warm and circled her nipples and found its way down the path of her belly. She felt his hands pull open her legs as he placed his mouth onto her willing pussy.

Michelle remembered he could eat pussy very well and recalled how his tongue sliding up and down her pussy sent pulses of sexual excitement throughout her body. She grabbed both of her large breasts and squeezed while the feel of his tongue rolling around between her pussy lips became pleasing and made her wet. She moaned and sighed at how well his tongue finds its way inside her fold and eventually turning the action into a performance of sucking her clit into his mouth and swallowing her juices. Michelle read how she squirmed and moaned as he sucked and bit on her pussy lips while stretching her soft legs wide open for his pleasure. Michelle grabbed his hair, pulling him close to her face and began to taste her pussy cum on his mouth while positioning him onto his back for her to return the favor.

She remembered how his balls were big and hung low while she grabbed his hard, leaking dick and forcing it deep into her wet mouth. She slid her mouth up and down his shaft while placing him deep into her throat, which allowed her to deep throat his entire cock. He was moaning and pulling her hair as she pulled off his hard dick and started to suck his large balls into her mouth aggressively. Michelle was excellent at allowing her hard nipples and big breasts to slide up and down a man's legs, adding different sensations of pleasure. She remembered how she rolled her tongue around his dick's head and could taste his precum leaking into her mouth and down her throat. She felt a pull of her hair and her body being positioned on her back as he held his hard dick in his hand and pulled open her legs.

Michelle could recall how his balls hang nicely as he pushed his hard dick head into her wet pussy while making her cry out in pleasure. His cock slid deep inside of her pussy while she began to move her hips up and down from the onset of fucking her deep. She positioned her legs upward and around his back while allowing her lover to have free access to every inch of her wet pussy. He began to move his body up and down on top of her while his mouth continued to suck her ample breast. She recalled how fast and hard he pumped her pussy and how her tits bounced back and forth as he rammed his dick deep inside her. She could feel and hear the wetness popping from her pussy juices as he forced his cock into her body. She loved recalling how his balls would bounce off her ass as he arched his penis in and out of her body. His deep fucking became faster as he started to feel his balls fell with warm cum.

Michelle could tell he was about to fill her wet pussy with thick, white cum and spread open even more to allow him to fuck her as fast and hard as he pleased. He let out a loud moan as he released a massive spurt of cum into Michelle's pussy hole. She felt the tingling and excitement of how her lover moaned and worshipped her pussy while releasing every drop of his seed deep into her body. He jerked and shot several waves of sperm into her body while biting and kissing Michelle's horny body. Michelle was excited how he used her pussy to please his hard dick and wrapped her legs tight around his body while using her pussy to tighten around his pulsing dick to drain every drop into her body. She slid her hips up and down as he shouted from the tickling while draining his balls completely.

As he slowed his movement, he fucked her slow while ending his run of pleasure deep in her body. He slipped his dick out of her pussy while rolling over onto the bed. Michelle remembered how his warm cum ran out of her pussy and down onto her ass, encouraging her to place her fingers inside her pussy to experience the feeling of cum on her fingers. She remembered how she put her fingers full of cum into her mouth and tasted his sperm. It was a little bitter but exciting when she felt the cum going into her mouth and down her throat. She noticed he had turned his back and did not communicate with her.

She started to reflect how men over the years have used her beautiful body for their sexual needs and never tried to comfort her or extend a hand of affection for a relationship. Michelle laid her diary down on her lap and thought about what happened after having a sexual encounter with other people. She reopened her diary, flipped a couple of years forward, and found a log where she was in a bookstore looking at books, and she accidentally turned into a man while walking about the aisle. The diary reminded her of a time where she went into a local bookstore, and while reading and moving a little toward, she left to grab another book, and her hand swung into the crotch area of an attractive man. Michelle said with an urgency that she was sorry and hoped she did not hurt him.

The man laughed and said, "I think everything is in place and hopefully still works properly."

Michelle noted the man paused as he caught sight of Michelle and looked mesmerized by her beauty. She said she had a short dress with a revealing low-cut top with cute sandals while her hair was free-flowing. Michelle read her notes that stated, "I was excited to catch the man repeatedly looking at my cleavage, and after a minute or two, I started to see his cock bulge in the front of his running pants."

"Today was a day that I felt good, energetic, and wanted to be a little naughty," said Michelle.

After making a short talk with the man concerning a couple of books, he asked her about another book while increasing his odds of continuing the conversation. Michelle caught wind of how he constantly looked at her breasts while heavily flirting that he was trying to come onto her; this made her feel good.

Michelle read her entry, stating she reached over and touched the man's arm regularly while sending a message she would be interested in something further. After reading this section, Michelle covered her mouth and thought about how she was too forward and should have tried controlling her sexual impulses much better. She continued to rediscover how she asked the man if he lived nearby, and he stated he did and was out on a personal day from work and thought he would try to find a couple of good books. The man reached up and touched Michelle's hair and stated how beautiful he thought she was and asked if she would like to come over to his house for a couple of drinks.

Michelle bit her lip and looked at the man and said, "I don't need drinks to do what I can do right here."

The man placed his finger on the side of her face and rubbed over her lips while sliding down to her gap between her large breasts. "Are you saying we can get to know each other right here and now?" asked the man.

Michelle looked over his shoulder and could not see any other guest within the aisle; she reached forward and squeezed his cock as he moved forward, kissing her lightly on her lips.

"I'm saying we're both adults, and I can make sure this big cock still works properly," said Michelle.

The man appeared surprised but willing and looked around and asked, "Right here, are you sure?"

Michelle knelt on her knees while looking up with her amazing brown eyes and slowly popped two buttons on her top, revealing her nice, rounded tits and asked him to stick his dick in her mouth. The man eagerly untied the front of his jogging pants and pulled out his hanging meat as Michelle quickly moved her mouth into position and opened wide, taking in almost the entire length of his cock deep into her soft mouth. The man's eyes rolled, and he gasped with pleasure while feeling her mouth tighten over his quickly hardening dick. Michelle moved her tongue aggressively around his dick while sliding her left hand around his body to cup his ass cheek. She moved her head back and forth while feeling his balls often smacking against her chin. The man could barely contain his moans of pleasure as he held onto Michelle's hair while helping her lovely mouth over his rock-hard shaft. Michelle felt the man trying to pull her away from his dick as she looked up and found he saw a person at the end of the long aisle with their back turned.

She became more excited and forcefully made him take it more rigid and faster with the effort of trying to make him unload into her mouth. The man gripped the back of Michelle's head, buried his mouth into the fold of his arm, and began to shake as Michelle felt a warm sensation of cum spurt onto her tongue. She popped and slurped his cumming cock as a couple of drips fell onto her exposed breast while the man tried hard not to scream from the onset of his load spilling out into her willing mouth. Michelle moved her tongue to the side, allowing his warm load to flow down her throat while consuming every drop from his deep well within his balls.

The man pulled his cock out of her mouth and softly squeezed the tip, allowing the excess cum to drop on her breasts as he told her how amazing she sucked a dick. He then turned to tie his pants, leaving Michelle alone as he quickly moved to another aisle in fear of being caught. Michelle turned and ran her finger over the cum drips and placed the cum on her tongue while enjoying the taste of fresh cum within her mouth. As she finished repositioning her breasts in her shirt, she walked over to the next aisle and tried to talk with the man who was nervously moving about and trying to walk away. Michelle read the note where she saw the man place his hand in his pocket, pulled a wedding ring out while putting back on his hand, and headed out the door. Reading the past event made Michelle realize events of her past and what she now had accepted as normal behavior was not the path she should be taking.

CHAPTER 11

Michelle turned and looked out her window while gazing with thought concerning how she had evolved from a typical woman who was relatively shy to a woman that allowed men to use her body as a fuck opportunity. She decided to continue reading a fond a memory that involved her at one of her best friend's parties. The journal entry explained how her friend, Emma, invited her over for a backyard grill out and party. She rediscovered the day was cool, and lots of people attended the party. Emma had several people from her family and a few from her work that participated in the event. Emma's husband controlled the grill while Emma entertained the guest and made sure everyone had a drink and was comfortable. Michelle remembered talking to several people, and as the night went on, she and many other people enjoyed laughing and consuming a mass number of mixed drinks. Later, as most people were leaving, Emma asked Michelle to stay the night from seeing Michelle stumbling and slurring from consuming a few too many drinks. Michelle agreed and hung tight with Emma as most guests said their goodbyes and headed home for the evening.

Emma and her husband finished cleaning up the evening offerings and helped Michelle find her way to the guest bedroom. Emma helped Michelle into her room and offered to supply her with some night clothing, but Michelle said she would sleep naked and laughed out loud. Emma thought Michelle was funny and told her to be careful about several other couples staying the night and not showing off her bare little butt.

As Emma shut Michelle's door, Michelle sat on the bedding and laid back for several minutes, trying to calm the feeling of her swimming from the onset of the alcohol. Michelle rose and began to take all her clothes off and wanted to lay nude on the bed and collect her thoughts while feeling the softness of the sheets against her nicely shaped body. She became bored and found a remote and flipped through several shows while finding nothing pleasing to her likeness. Michelle caught sight of bathing suits and robes hanging on the other side of the room and recalled Emma had a hot tub. She walked over to the robe and tried it on; it fit perfectly, and she decided to find the hot tub and soak in the warmth and bubbles for some time. She exited the room and continued to the side of the house where the hot tub was located and found a guest was in the hot tub submerged up to his neck while his head was tilted back. The door clicked behind her, alerting the man of her presence, and Michelle said, "Sorry, I did not mean to bother you, I was going to soak up the hot tub for a while before bed. I'll come back later," said Michelle.

The man looked and smiled at Michelle and asked, "Is your name, Michelle?"

Michelle said yes and looked at him for a moment and said, "You're Aaron from Emma's place of work, right?"

The man said, "Yes, you're free to join me if you like, but I will need to confess, I do not have clothing on."

Michelle, feeling a little frisky and absorbed with alcohol, giggled and said "No worries" and dropped her robe entirely in front of Aaron and revealed her amazing body while entering the hot tub.

Michelle remembered how Aaron was surprised and gazed at the beauty of her body as she entered the water. Aaron watched as Michelle slowly entered the hot tub while becoming familiar with the water's warm temperatures. He was almost speechless as he gazed at Michelle's perfectly manicured heart-shaped pubic hairs and could not resist the temptation to soak in the fantastic size of her double-D breasts that sparkled with nipple piercings. As Michelle continued to lower her body down into the water, she felt the force of the jets briefly tickle her pussy.

"Would you like a glass of wine?" asked Aaron.

Michelle declined the offer and asked, "Did you enjoy the party? And who was the woman you were talking with when I arrived and met with Emma?"

Aaron smiled and said her name was Amber, and they met a few weeks prior at a business meeting.

"She is beautiful," said Michelle.

Michelle heard the click of the door behind her and turned her head while discovering Amber was walking toward the hot tub. Michelle felt awkward and began to wonder if there would be a problem with her nude in the hot tub with Amber's boyfriend.

"Hi, honey, this is Michelle who wanted to relax for a few in the hot tub. I told her it's okay," said Aaron.

"You're Michelle, right?" asked Amber while kneeling next to Michelle outside the hot tub with a T-shirt, flip-flops, and a new bottle of wine.

"Yes, I saw you with Aaron earlier but not sure we have met," said Michelle.

"We haven't. I'm Amber Zelensky, a business partner of Emma's company," said Amber. Amber reached out her hand and shook hands with Michelle saying, "More the merrier when it's a hot-tub party."

Michelle observed Amber pull her T-shirt over her flowing red hair while revealing her rounded and perky breast. Her skin was creamy color with a bit of tan, and when she stepped into the water, Michelle could see many colorful tattoos flowing from her arms, chest, hips, and down her legs. Her vagina area was smooth and not a hair to be seen with some piercing dangling from her clitoris. Amber's fingertips and toenails were painted black while posing dark shading around her eyes that highlighted her beauty.

Michelle continued to read her journal entry and remembered how attractive and exotic Amber appeared to her. Amber was high-strung and laughed loudly as they continued in small talk, making Michelle laugh more than she has in a long while.

"Do you have any tattoos, Michelle?" asked Amber.

"No, to be honest, I have always liked them but too chicken because of the pain," explained Michelle.

"I can assure you, it's not near as bad as you think, and to be truthful, some were erotic," said Amber.

"What do you mean by erotic?" asked Michelle.

"Do you mind if I show you my body up closer?" asked Amber.

"Please I'm curious," stated Michelle.

Amber stood up and sat on the back of the hot tub and revealed the side tattoo that Michelle caught a quick look at earlier. The tattoo ran from her back and around her side while leading to the top of her vagina. "I received this ink several years ago, and during the time, I was actively experimenting with Molly, and when the artist was working around my pussy, the sensations mixed with slight pain sent me into an orgasm that was an extreme pleasure. We had to stop the tattoo momentarily while I cleaned up my wet pussy," explained Amber.

"You're lying," excitedly cried Michelle.

"Nope, I swear it," said Amber as she took a drink of her wine.

"I have to ask, what about the piercing in your pussy?" asked Michelle.

"No, that just fucking hurt but feels good now when my lover flicks it with his tongue," excitedly explained Amber. "Do you want to see it?" asked Amber.

Michelle paused for a moment and said, "Uh, yes, if you don't mind."

Amber pulled open her legs, and she leaned back her hands on the flooring, revealing a piercing through her pink-colored opening that appeared to be a gold ring with some charm hanging from the loop. "It's a four-leaf clover if you're wondering," explained Amber. "It's magically delicious," said Amber as everyone let out a rolling-belly laugh.

"What about you, Michelle, I know you said there are no tattoos, but do you have any piercings?" asked Amber?

"I do," explained Michelle. Michelle lifted her body out of the water and revealed her pierced nipples that displayed a little silver bar that ran from right to left centered in her nipples.

"Wow, you have fantastic breasts, and are they real?" asked Amber.

"Yes, 100 percent natural," said Michelle.

"I don't believe you," said Amber.

Michelle stood up and revealed her heart-shaped pubic hairs that Amber thought were amazing as well and said, "Here, touch them if you don't believe me."

Amber said, "Okay," and approached Michelle and placed both her hands on her breast and smiled while squeezing and rubbing while then said, "What the fuck, they are real and perfect."

Amber slipped back and submerged her body in the fizzing water while getting close to Aaron, who was overly excited by witnessing the actions of two hot women within the same area he sat naked. "Someone is hard as a rock between their legs. It's time for you to show us what you have since we both have shared our bodies," said Amber.

Aaron stood up slowly, and Michelle locked her eyes immediately on his dick that was thick and curved with tight balls extended at full length before her eyes.

Amber laughed and grabbed his dick and said "Someone is enjoying the sight of our guest a little too much" as she stroked it a couple of times and looked at Michelle and smiled.

Aaron revealed a lower back tattoo that was positioned in the area just above his ass. Michelle thought the tattoo was odd-looking and not in the proper place for a man but said "Looks nice" to be respectful.

Amber laughed and smacked his lower back, saying, "Tramp stamp, I bet your boy lovers pop all over your sissy tattoo."

Aaron laughed and said, "You haven't complained before."

Amber giggled and said, "No, I like to watch a stud tear up your little ass."

Michelle laughed loudly as Amber continued to tease her boyfriend about guys fucking him in his ass. "That is the one thing I have not watched," said Michelle.

"What, a guy being fucked in the ass?" asked Amber.

"Yes, a guy fucking a guy," said Michelle.

"Honey, it's erotic and stimulating all at the same time." Amber moved closer to Michelle and whispered in her ear, "It's enjoyable when a guy fucks Aaron in his ass while he sucks on my pussy."

Michelle recalled how she began to become excited at the thought of the actions and felt a tingling in her pussy when she gazed at Amber when she talked dirty. As they spoke, Amber would consistently move closer and began placing her hands on her legs and playing with Michelle's hair, which started a thirst deep in Michelle to kiss Amber. Michelle had never been this tempted to kiss a girl but was increasingly becoming more excited the more they conversed. Amber continued to talk about how pretty Michelle's hair was and noticed Aaron creeping up behind her, rubbing her back and eventually moving around to squeeze her breasts.

Amber placed her hand on Michelle's face and asked if she would be comfortable kissing Aaron. Michelle said yes, and Aaron positioned himself in front of Michelle and began to place his warm lips onto hers while Michelle felt the soft hand on Amber rubbing her breast and making its way down to the inner portion on her leg. Michelle gave in and allowed the couple to explore her willing body as Aaron slipped his tongue into her mouth while she felt Amber touched her pussy which sent pulses of desire throughout her body. Amber pushed Aaron out of the way while he grabbed Amber from behind and forced his cock into her ass. Amber found her way to Michelle's mouth, deeply kissing her with her soft lips and aggressively figured Michelle's pussy clit.

Amber cried out, "Fuck, his dick is thick," and whispered in Michelle's ear that he was slipping slowly into her ass.

Michelle was burned with curiosity and desire as she saw Aaron slowly pushing his dick into Amber's ass while holding tightly onto her hips. Amber's tongue found its way through Michelle's face and neck area as Michelle pulled herself from the water and sat on the edge while spreading her legs wide open. Michelle gasped as Amber pulled opened her fold and began to lick up and down her wet clit. Michelle recalled how she leaned back on one arm and placed her right hand on Amber's head, feeling the force of Aaron fucking her ass and feeling Amber moan loudly in and out as Aaron's fucking became faster and deeper within her perfect ass.

"Fuck my ass, bitch!" screamed Amber as Michelle witnessed how much Aaron enjoyed fucking her ass.

Michelle felt intense sucking and pressure from the onset of Amber's mouth slurping up her flowing juices. Michelle's eyes watered with pleasure as she reached up and rubbed her breasts while enjoying the presence of a woman devouring her horny pussy.

What the fuck, thought Michelle. She loved men but quickly realized a man could not pleasure her pussy as a woman could. Michelle began to shake and promptly realized she was about to cum all over this beautiful redhead's mouth.

She let out a loud burst of air and gripped Amber's hair tightly while burying her mouth firmly onto her pussy and released a rush of pussy fluids followed by body jerks of orgasms into Amber's mouth that consumed all her wetness. Michelle pushed Amber back to relieve her instant tickling and saw her pussy fluids stringing from Amber's mouth as she continued to witness Aaron fucking the living hell out of her asshole. Amber positioned her hand left and right of Michelle on the hot tub and placed her head between Michelle's breast as Aaron was in full speed deep in her ass. Amber whimpered and moaned with pleasure as she rubbed her face over Michelle's ample breast. Aaron began to moan loudly as he thrust his dick into Amber's ass while stopping balls deep and then repeating, again and again, until he dumped every drop of his load deep into her willing ass. Amber yelled and moaned as she enjoyed her lover pumping fresh cum into her ass while pushing Michelle's body back and biting on the inner portions of her legs. Aaron pulled out of Amber while his dick dripped thick white cum onto the colored tattoos on Amber's back and removed himself from the hot tub.

Amber began to aggressively jack herself off while biting on Michelle's pussy lips and inner leg areas. After a few seconds, Amber pulled her head up and revealed her flushed red body aggressively jerking off while her eyes became glossed over and her tongue pushing against the side of her mouth. She displayed a straining look as her veins filled with blood within her neck while dropping her head into a screaming sound that released deep waves of pleasure and orgasms from her pussy.

Amber pulled her head up, allowing Michelle to witness her increased breathing patterns and running eye mascara from the onset of her pussy, releasing waves of pleasure throughout her body. Michelle pushed her body directly down into the water and pulled Amber on top of her in a mounting position while placing two fingers within Amber's wet, swollen pussy and sucking her perky breasts. Amber slowly moved her hips back and forth, fucking Michelle's fingers while sucking and biting Michelle's lips. Michelle was lost within this moment and found deep satisfaction from discovering a woman's soft body. Michelle ran her left hand around and cupped Amber's firm round ass as she found leverage to force her fingers even deeper into Amber's wet pussy, which sent Amber into a wild state.

Together with Michelle's efforts, Amber turned into a deep, penetrating experience that allowed Michelle to experience the state of how wet Amber's clean-shaven pussy could become. While Amber aggressively fucked Michelle's fingers, she pulled her hair back forcefully. She bit Michelle's shoulder area hard, sending Michelle into waves of erotic pleasure while Michelle felt Amber's pussy charm sliding up and down her fingers. Their breast nipples consistently rub each other, and the softness of their skin became a never-ending memory of pleasure. As Amber slowed her hip thrust over Michelle's fingers, they embraced several minutes and participated in deep, sensual kissing before parting ways.

After reading her journal entries, Michelle found herself within a deep state of arousal and began to think of Xavier and his gentle approach to her. Sex with others was fun beyond measure, but something was missing from her journal entries, and the feeling ran deep within Michelle with a longing for a singular mate. Michelle continued to stare out her window and closed the journal on her lap while thinking about what life would be like to be with a person who respected her and loved her beyond her body. Michelle rubbed her hands against her face, departed from her bedroom, and stood at her kitchen counter. She thought deeply about her evening with Xavier and looked forward to their date at her place.

This has to be perfect, thought Michelle. She began to open her pantry and pull out her best dinnerware while elegantly prepping her table. She placed fine china on her table left to her by her grandmother and glasses so clear they appeared transparent. She folded each napkin perfectly and made sure wrinkles did not appear as she laid out freshly polished silverware. Michelle positioned each item to mirror the other side in a perfect presentation while finishing up the table with a candelabrum directly in the center of the table. The tablecloth was gray, the napkins were colored with a mixture of yellow and reds, while the candelabrum displayed white candles.

Perfect, thought Michelle. The easy part was done, but what to cook for dinner made Michelle nervous.

CHAPTER 12

Michelle grabbed her purse and excitedly rushed out of her apartment, sporting a T-shirt, short shorts, and flip-flops while in pursuit of creating the best meal for Xavier. Michelle stepped out of her apartment complex and started to walk a couple of blocks to the local supermarket. She smiled as several construction workers hurled provocative comments and whistled at her. Michelle found how men adored her looks, and the attention has always exited her. *Michelle, get a grip today and focus,* thought Michelle.

As much as she loved the attention, she did realize how she dressed and had grown accustomed to wearing shirts that were tight around her double-D breast size without a bra and shorts that are so small her ass cheeks flex as she walked. Thoughts of change kept entering into her mind as she pondered how she needed to dress appropriately tonight and make an excellent impression. Michelle entered the grocery store and overheard, "Good afternoon, Michelle, how are you today?" asked by the young college-aged bagger who always made it a point to hit on Michelle.

"I'm doing just fine, Justin. How is your girlfriend?" asked Michelle to draw the attention off her. She had discovered that when she made it known he had a girlfriend, he will back off his flirtatious advances.

Michelle pondered on what the menu should consist of tonight and became nervous once again when faced with the challenge of cooking a meal to impress her date. *Ding,* sounded from her phone within her purse. Michelle pulled her phone and instantly became excited to see a text from Xavier that read, "I have thought a lot about you today and look forward to visiting your apartment and enjoying a date with you tonight, have a great day, I will see you promptly at 7:00 p.m."

Michelle smiled as she continued to soak in the new attention she received from Xavier and began to realize he could be someone extraordinary in her life. "I am looking forward to spending the evening with you as well, Xavier," texted Michelle while adding an emoji face that sent a wink.

Michelle stepped into the bathroom for a brief moment, and when she was finished, she caught sight of how good she looked from the onset of wearing provocative clothing that attracted almost every man. She stood in the mirror and imagined Xavier watching her from across the room while pulling up her shirt and releasing her ample breast, revealing their sexy shape and hardened nipples. "Xavier, do you like what you see?" imagined Michelle. As much as Michelle wanted to be proper, she also wanted to be very bad with Xavier.

Michelle walked out of the bathroom while passing a middle-aged man who smiled and looked at her up and down while passing by. Michelle could not resist the urge to stop and bend over while pretending to grab a box on the lower shelf. She caught sight of the man's eyes staring intensely on her well-shaped ass and enjoyed the fact she could have his dick if she wanted. Michelle stopped for a moment, stood up, and quickly crossed over into the next aisle with much regret that she could not control her urges to be what she had become for so many years. "What am I doing, and why do I keep throwing myself out there for every man and woman to salivate over?" asked Michelle while in deep thought.

She realized she was standing in the magazine aisle and caught sight of a book that had a picture of a woman and man sitting in front of a beautiful log cabin with the title saying, "Happiness in marriage is for everyone." Michelle turned the pages and began to explore the article's contents, which gave several tips on attracting your mate and keeping your mate happy within a marriage. She noticed the article never mentioned dressing sexy in public to entice your mate or provided information about relationships built on random sex acts with people. Michelle was accustomed to sex stories throughout her day and provided advice on connecting with their partners but lacked relationship-building techniques when trying to form a relationship.

Michelle had become isolated within her world that involved many sexual partners with extended sexual acts that shield her fallacies. She pondered the picture of the woman and man sitting while embracing and smiling and wondered if that could be her one day. She imagined the image revealing her and Xavier and thought how it would be just settling down with one man and making a life that laughing and loving children would surround. She closed the magazine and placed it in her cart and proceeded to the meat section.

"Michelle, how are you?" asked a voice behind her.

Michelle turned around and saw it was one of her old friends she had not seen in a few years. Michelle asked how she was doing and caught an awkward sight out of the side of her eye. Michelle tried to retain her bubbly approach as her old friend's husband walked up and viciously eyed her appearance.

"Carl and I have decided to have another baby," explained the friend.

"I'm very happy for you both," said Michelle as she saw Carl staring deep into her eyes. Michelle felt awkward because she spent the night at her friend's home one night after their party and allowed Carl to fuck her on the sofa late at night while her friend was asleep upstairs. Michelle's last memory of Carl was when he pulled out of her and shot his load onto her bare chest as he quickly scrambled to clean up and try not to be caught by his wife.

"Why did we stop spending time together?" asked her friend.

"You know, life just gets busier and busier," explained Michelle. The real reason was buried in Michelle's guilty conscience where she was disappointed that she allowed herself to give in to Carl's sexual pursuit while betraying her best friend.

"Yea, Michelle, we would love to have you back over," said Carl with the devilish look of intentions.

Michelle's friend grabbed her and gave her a big hug and said, "Please call me some time. I would love to hang out with you."

Her betrayal on her best friend saddened Michelle, and when her friend hugged her, she noticed Carl gave her a wink that made her feel uncomfortable. As they departed, Michelle embarked on her mission to quickly grab what she needed and make her way out of the store. When Michelle crossed over into another aisle, she found Carl had slipped away from her friend and approached her.

"You look fucking good, girl. Can we hook up again?" asked Carl.

"Carl, what we have done was a mistake, and I should have never slept with my best friend's husband, so, no, we can never do that again," whispered Michelle.

"Fuck you, you slut, I got that pussy and came on those awesome tits. You weren't complaining when I was deep in your wet pussy!" rudely shouted Carl.

Michelle felt a rush of adrenaline and anger sweeping through her body as she felt terrible for what she had done and how Carl spoke to her like she was nothing. She quickly headed back to the meat aisle. While trying to hold in her tears, she began to shake and wanted just to run away from everything. *Ding*, sounded her phone as she aggressively looked, frustrated, thinking Carl was texting her more insults, and noticed Xavier sent another message. At that moment, Michelle felt a soothing feeling as she became entangled within Xavier's message.

"I do not want to sound creepy or weird, but I miss you and can't wait to meet up with you tonight, have a great day," texted Xavier.

Michelle felt confidence and strength release throughout her body while grabbing the best-cut steaks the store had to offer. She continued to regain focus, blocking out the things she has done, and concentrated on building a menu. Michelle decided to grab two big potatoes and threw in ingredients for a Caesar salad. She also found a cherry pie she could warm up and add a scoop of vanilla ice cream to top off the evening. As she approached the counter, she noticed several bottles of wine and decided to grab an upscale brand that she liked.

Michelle found her way back to her apartment and sat the bags on the table and leaned against the wall with her hands over her face. She felt terrible how Carl brought back her feelings of disappointment and treated her like she was a piece of ass that was only good for fucking. *I can't believe I allowed him to fuck me in my best friend's house on her sofa*, sadly thought Michelle.

Michelle recalled how Carl was charming and consistently flirted with her throughout the evening. Later while at her friend's home, after everyone was in bed and she was on the sofa, Carl came down and asked her if he could talk to her. Carl went into much detail about how he wanted to make his sex life better with her friend while Michelle provided many techniques and ways to improve his pursuit. Michelle remembered how Carl had nothing on but shorts and displayed a well-cut body she found attractive. As the talking continued late into the night, Michelle became weak and lay back on the sofa while pulling up her leg that exposed her panties and asked Carl if he wanted to try some of his newfound techniques. Carl glanced up the stairs and moved in toward Michelle's pussy and sucked on the outside of her panties while finding his way to her breasts. He quickly pulled her panties off and aggressively jerked her shirt off and positioned his cock in the front of Michelle's mouth, where she willingly took his length into her wet mouth.

Michelle remembered how the interaction was exciting from the possibility of being caught while giving in to her desire to fuck Carl. He allowed Michelle to suck him for several minutes and then pulled open her soft legs and shoved his cock quickly into her pussy. Michelle remembered he was like a wild animal that fucked aggressively and hard while obsessing over her large breasts. The fast fucking lasted only two minutes as he pulled out of Michelle's pussy and shot his thick load onto her breasts. She remembered how he did not say a word and quickly ran off to cover his wrongdoings. Michelle made her way into their guest bathroom, where she reflected, looking into the mirror with both hands on the sink while covered in cum and feeling very disappointed by her actions. She grabbed toilet paper, began to clean off her best friend's husband's seed from her chest area, packed up her things, and went back home to never speak with them until today.

Michelle wiped the tears from her eyes as she recalled the events of her past and how she had formed a life that was structured around temptation, lust, and fucking whoever she desired.

CHAPTER 13

Michelle placed the two potatoes into the oven and prepared the Caesar salad. She headed back to her bedroom, where she prepared a hot bath, undressed, and sunk her body into the water. Michelle tried hard to clear her thoughts concerning her troubling and promiscuous past. Her thoughts began to center back on Xavier, and she began to smile as she recalled the kindness and events of the evening he shared with her prior. She bathed her body with soaps that contained fragrances of pears and washed her hair with shampoo that projected the odor of freshness. As she padded the water from her bath from her body, she rubbed fine oils into her skin that were well-pleasing to the smell. She applied her makeup with deep detail and fashioned her brunette hair into lovely curls that flowed down her back. Michelle gazed into her closet at the vast number of dresses and pulled the black dress that covered her shoulders but left just enough cleavage view for the imagination. She slipped on her red Victoria's Secret bra, matching panties, and unrolled her black thigh pantyhose up her nicely shaved legs. Michelle grabbed her robe and proceeded to head back to the kitchen, where she pulled the baked potatoes and seared the thick rib eyes over olive oil and rosemary. Michelle noticed the time was slipping away and only had about fifteen minutes until Xavier was scheduled to arrive.

Michelle placed the cooked rib eyes on the plates while slicing the potatoes and scooping the Caesar salad into bowls. She put each item onto the table perfectly and covered each dish with a silver lid while rushing back to the bedroom. She sprayed her body with Love Spell body spray and slipped her red high heels. She heard a knock at the front door and felt a rush of nervousness sweep across her body. She cautiously walked quickly to the door and took a deep breath while she fluffed her hair one more time while opening it to discover Xavier standing with flowers and a big smile. Michelle noticed he was dressed in a plaid shirt with jeans and brown shoes while wearing a dark-colored blazer.

"Thank you for inviting me tonight, Michelle. These flowers are for you," said Xavier as he handed the flowers to Michelle and leaned in gave her a light kiss on her cheek. "Wow, you smell amazing while glaring with beauty," explained Xavier.

"Thank you, you look nice too. Would you like to come in?" asked Michelle.

Xavier walked into Michelle's apartment and commented how he loved her big windows and the view she had overlooking the city.

"Will you please have a seat while I will finish putting together supper?" asked Michelle.

Xavier smiled and sat down on Michelle's sofa and looked at several pics she had hanging on her wall. He noticed Michelle in pictures with several people and asked if the images were her family.

"Yes, the picture above the fireplace is me with my parents and my siblings while the other pics are friends," explained Michelle.

Xavier noticed how beautiful Michelle's smile was and became impressed with her beauty within the photos. He stood up and looked out the window and viewed people walking while cars passed through the streets. It appeared that Michelle lives about eight to nine stories above the city while the view seemed to go on for many miles. As Xavier stood looking out into the vast amount of city buildings, he heard from behind "Hi, would you like a glass of wine while you take in the view" asked by Michelle while handing Xavier a glass half-filled with red wine.

"Thank you," said Xavier. "I do enjoy the beauty of the city but love the county environment to where I can be free and break away from people," explained Xavier.

Michelle enjoyed Xavier being with her at this moment and started to become lost in his gentle voice and watching him hold the glass and place it next to his lips while speaking about things that make him happy.

"What is that building over there?" said Xavier while pointing toward a tall building out in the distance.

"I believe that is a hotel," replied Michelle.

"Such a tall building for a hotel," said Xavier.

"Would you like to join me for dinner now?" asked Michelle.

"I would love that. Please show me the way," said Xavier.

Michelle took Xavier by the hand, gave him a gentle smile while leading him to the kitchen, and asked him to please sit while preparing the final stages. Michelle uncovered the silver-plate topper, revealing a nice golden-brown steak with a baked potato steamed lightly with melted butter with a side of Caesar salad.

Michelle walked back over to the stove, removed hot bread from the oven, and placed it in the middle of the table, surrounded by olive oil, grated cheese, and room-temperature butter.

"Michelle, the dinner looks and smells amazing. You did not have to go through this much trouble for me," explained Xavier.

Michelle said, "No trouble at all. I wanted to prepare a nice dinner for tonight."

Michelle suddenly remembered the events of the supermarket and Carl's disgusting comments that almost ruined the evening, but the sight of Xavier sitting at her table and preparing to eat her food was pleasing. Xavier began to eat by placing his napkin on his lap and making sure his left hand rested on his knee. Michelle watched and noticed Xavier looking at her while realizing he was waiting for her to take the first bite. Michelle positioned her napkin and body and placed her fork into the Caesar salad while taking in the first bite. She noticed Xavier followed her actions and began eating his salad and cutting his steak.

"I hope the steak is pleasing to your liking," said Michelle.

Xavier looked directly into Michelle's eyes and said, "Everything tonight is pleasing to me," while smiling.

Michelle almost melted in her seat and suddenly asked if he would please excuse her for a moment. Michelle quickly walked back to her bedroom and started to cry and found herself overwhelmed with Xavier's kindness. She stood there for a moment, regained her emotions, and made sure her makeup was okay while returning to the table.

"Michelle, are you okay?" asked Xavier.

"Yes, I'm fine and more than fine to see you sitting at my table. Please forgive me, it's been a difficult day," explained Michelle.

"This potato is the best I have eaten in a long time," stated Xavier.

"Potato, the potato is the best you have eaten," replied Michelle as she started to laugh at Xavier's humor.

"Oh, and this steak, wow, it's the best cut of meat I have ever tasted along with this wonderful display of bread and salad," excitedly explained Xavier.

"You haven't reached the dessert yet. It will knock your socks off," jokingly said Michelle.

"If the dessert is half as lovely as the host, then I'm in trouble," said Xavier.

Michelle froze and struggled with all her might to not jump up and physically take over Xavier's body. "You are the sweetest man I ever met," said Michelle.

Xavier smiled and finished up his plate while thanking Michelle for the delightful dinner.

"Are you ready for a dessert?" asked Michelle.

"More than ready," replied Xavier.

Michelle stood up while Xavier marveled at her beauty as she walked toward the kitchen. Xavier took a deep breath as he tried to control his nervousness and thought about how lucky he was to be here with the most beautiful woman he had ever met.

Michelle opened the door from the kitchen while returning with a sliced cherry pie that had a scoop of vanilla ice cream melting over the crust onto the plate.

"This looks delicious, thank you," said Xavier. "When I was a child, my grandmother would bake desserts, and when I would enter her home, it was the best memory that still exists in my mind," said Xavier.

"I hope my pie is well-tasty for your pleasure, Xavier," said Michelle with a wink.

Xavier choked a little while taking a bite from the sensual gesture Michelle threw his way and grabbed his drink to wash down the pie.

"Are you okay?" asked Michelle.

"Yes, yes, sorry, I took too big of a bite," explained Xavier. Xavier lied about the cause of his misshape at Michelle's table. The absolute truth was embedded in his suddenly dirty thought that flashed within his imagination as Michelle asked if her pie was pleasing to him.

Michelle looked at Xavier with her cute little crooked smile and took another bite from becoming the champion of making Xavier think dirty. Michelle was pleased that Xavier displayed a realm of innocence and extended himself well beyond the normal gentleman.

Xavier and Michelle spoke for several minutes more about family and regular, daily routines while finishing up the bottle of wine and dessert. Xavier helped Michelle clean up the remains of dinner while straightening up the kitchen, and while he stood alongside Michelle at the sink, things became quiet. Xavier passed dishes to Michelle as she took a towel and removed the water while placing them back into their proper location. Xavier would take a peek at Michelle, and she would smile back at him when she noticed he was looking at her. Xavier felt a heaviness within his chest and a feeling he was unfamiliar with while engaging with Michelle.

I'm falling for this woman, thought Xavier. *This woman is amazing and perfect while I enjoy everything about her*, Xavier's thoughts continue.

Now and then, Xavier's hand would brush Michelle's hand while the interaction would send goose bumps across his arms. Meanwhile, Michelle was speechless, which was uncommon. She realized she thought Xavier was fantastic and wanted to change who she was and won him over but afraid he might think badly of her concerning her promiscuous past once he became familiar with who she was and what she had done.

"Done," said Michelle. "Would you like a tour of my apartment?" asked Michelle, trying to break the silence.

"I would love to," said Xavier.

Michelle took Xavier's hand and led him into the living room, saying, "You have already seen this room, but I will take you to my bedroom."

Xavier suddenly felt an extreme sense of attraction toward Michelle as they walked into her bedroom. The bedroom was lovely, with a dark green color and oakwood flooring. Xavier caught a scent of Michelle's body sprays within the area that sent pulses of desire streaking through his body. Michelle continued to pull Xavier along into her bathroom as he caught sight of her bear-claw bathtub while visually observing her surroundings. Xavier enjoyed Michelle's sense of style and found her home contained many beautiful pieces of artwork. As Michelle continued to lead Xavier by holding his hand, he stopped while pulling her around close toward his body.

"I'm sorry, but I need to do this," said Xavier.

Michelle stood as her eyes became more expansive and wondered what he was going to do. Xavier took her other hand, leaned forward, and kissed Michelle lightly on her lips while pulling her close to his body. Michelle's body was almost like putty in the hands of an artist as she embraced the warmth and feel of Xavier's body.

The kisses became deeper as Xavier placed his hand on the exposed area of Michelle's back that showed through her dress. Michelle began to become overfilled with a burning desire to rip open Xavier's shirt and push him back onto the bedding. Still, Michelle restrained her temptation to take Xavier as she felt his tongue slip into her mouth while finding hers. The sensation sent waves of acceptance as she opened her mouth wider to take more of Xavier's soft tongue. Michelle felt her pussy tickle while feeling the pressure of Xavier's cock becoming hard in his pants and pushing up against her belly. Michelle tightly wrapped her arms around Xavier's body as he pushed her up against the wall and ran his warm tongue down the side of her neck.

Take me now, thought Michelle, who was internally begging for Xavier to pull open her legs and wrap them around his body while fucking her against the wall. She burned with desire as he squeezed the side of her hip and deeply kissed her willing body. Michelle felt Xavier pull back while placing both hands on her face and giving her a gentle kiss on her forehead while embracing her with a tight hug.

Again, are you serious? thought Michelle as she wondered why he began to take her and then restrained her from going farther.

Xavier said sorry while grabbing her by the hand; he directed her toward the living room and asked her to sit with him.

"Michelle, I have had the best evening, and I need to tell you something," said Xavier.

Michelle became tense and expected Xavier to tell her that he did not want to see her and needed to leave.

Xavier looked at Michelle's eyes and said, "I think you are unique, kind, beautiful, and beyond perfect. I would like to take things slow if that's okay with you." Xavier continued to explain how he was beginning to develop deep feelings for Michelle and did not want to mess things up by moving too fast. "I was raised to respect women and to do things in a certain order, I will not sit here and tell you that I'm a saint and have not made mistakes, but my mistakes are why I do not want to mess this up," explained Xavier.

Michelle felt an unusual feeling deep inside her body as she remembered her mother telling her many years ago that she will know when she meets the right man, and that sense will help guide her. Michelle understood what her mother was telling her, placed her hands on Xavier's knees, and said, "So does this make me your girlfriend?"

Xavier laughed and hugged Michelle while whispering in her ear, "Would you like to be my girlfriend?"

Michelle pulled her head back and felt a feeling of youthfulness flowing through her body and said "Yes" while realizing Xavier was for real.

Michelle's past and sexual routine begin to flash through the depths of her mind as she embarked on a new journey that was magical and almost unreal. She started to feel what might be love, and the person sitting in front of her maybe that person who her mother said would present himself to her one day, and on that day, her life would suddenly change forever.

"I know the girlfriend routine is a bit corny, but I like you and want to get to know you much better," said Xavier.

Michelle thought for a second and realized that something different might be exactly what her life needed. "Xavier, your words are perfect," said Michelle.

Xavier leaned forward and kissed Michelle on her soft cheek and said, "This evening was the best, and I cannot wait until we can see each other again. I feel as if I have known you for years."

Xavier stood up and said he must head back home and get some sleep.

Michelle walked Xavier to the door and said, "You gave me a perfect evening when I needed it the most, and thank you for coming over."

Xavier reached out and ran his finger into her hair while parting her hair over her ear and said, "I'll call you tomorrow if that's okay?" asked Xavier.

"Yes, that would be nice. I'll be expecting your call," replied Michelle as Xavier walked out the door. Michelle closed the door and knelt on her knees with her back against the closed door and ran her hands through her hair while smiling bigger than she had in a long while.

CHAPTER 14

Michelle went to her room to turn in for the night and add today's events in her journal. She wrote how she was excited about the night and the interaction with her friend's husband, Carl, while finishing up details concerning the evening with Xavier and how she thought she was starting to fall in love with him. Michelle sat for a time and thought long about Xavier and the events throughout her life. Some were good memories, but a lot was filled with wrong choices and careless actions. *Why have I made so many bad decisions?* thought Michelle.

She decided to put away her journal and think about good things. Michelle thought about how nice Xavier looked and how well he treated her with the utmost amount of respect. Even though she was frustrated concerning sexual intercourse with Xavier, she decided to give this a chance and see where it took them. Still, the evening circumstances did not change because Michelle was sexually frustrated without Xavier's dick around to please her. *I could easily take care of this by calling up one of my past lovers or simply going down the bar and finding a willing partner,* thought Michelle. *No, no, no, this kind of behavior has to end, and it's time to start a new path,* thought Michelle. *Ah, I know just how to take care of this,* pondered Michelle.

Michelle stood up and dropped her sexy dress on the floor while she kicked off her high heels. She removed all her clothing but her Victoria's Secret black thigh-high pantyhose. Her breast felt extra perky, and she had no doubt her pussy was wet and needing to be filled. She lay back onto her bed and spread her legs open, revealing her heart-shaped hair pattern above her pink pussy folds. Her nipples had piercings of petite flowers in the color of pink, while her toenals and fingernails were painted bright red. She cupped her breast with both hands and squeezed her round portions as her hands slipped to the inner sections of her thighs. She moved her right hand over her perfectly heart-shaped pussy hairs and then pulled open her fold while finding her erect clit. She gasped as her finger rubbed in a circular motion over her sweet spot while sending pulses of pleasure throughout her body. Her thoughts centered on the memory of seeing Xavier stroking his big dick on his couch while she snooped secretly in his kitchen. At that moment, she wanted to be there, mounting his dick and placing his hands on her large breast as she grinded her pussy back and forth, making him moan in pleasure.

Michelle about jumped out of her bed when she heard her phone suddenly ring beside her. She grabbed the phone without seeing who was calling and said "Hello" in a stubborn voice.

"Oh, hi, did I call at a bad time?" asked Xavier.

Michelle sat up quickly on the side of her bed while throwing her hair back and pleaded. "No, I thought you were one of those annoying sales calls," said Michelle while quickly creating a story to cover up her frustration while being disturbed during masturbation.

"I was thinking about you and hoped you do not find me as creepy, but I could not sleep while my mind kept racing with the thought of you," said Xavier.

"I will admit, I was doing the same thing while lying in bed trying to force myself to sleep, but the evening was perfect, and I'm glad you had dinner with me," explained Michelle.

"How do you sleep?" asked Xavier.

Michelle thought for a second and was confused by the question but answered, "In a bed."

Xavier laughed and said, "Silly, I mean, what is your routine?"

Michelle let out a giggle while Xavier quickly responded how he thought her voice was sexy and stimulating.

Michelle began to blush slightly and told Xavier how she usually ran a hot bath while surrounding herself with candles. She explained how she liked to submerge in the water and drown out all the troubles of the day. "I listen to many different stories, some are interesting while a lot are negative," explained Michelle.

"I get it," said Xavier. "Many days I have to force myself to set aside all the mess I discover within our town and have to tell myself to keep it at work," said Xavier. "I jump on my four-wheeler and just ride for hours throughout the countryside while stopping and fishing on and off at my favorite areas," said Xavier.

"I enjoyed the four-wheel ride with you, Xavier," stated Michelle.

"Anytime you want to ride, you are always welcomed, just ask, and I will make it happen," said Xavier.

"I bet all your past girls loved the four-wheeler rides," said Michelle.

"No, you are the first girl I have taken out on my four-wheeler," said Xavier.

Michelle became more excited as she closed her eyes and listened to the sound of Xavier's voice and discreetly touched her body in various places.

"What else do you do after you take a hot bath? I must know," bravely stated Xavier.

"Xavier, I think you are flirting with me over the phone," said Michelle.

"Is that okay?" stated Xavier as the conversation paused for a few seconds.

"Yes, I feel like a teenager talking over the phone late at night. This is fun," said Michelle.

Michelle began to explain how she took her baths and then rubbed her body from top to bottom with lotions while slipping on nothing but a shirt.

"I'm speechless," said Xavier. "It was all I could do when you stayed at my home to control my eyes when you wore my clothing," stated Xavier.

"Why did you feel you needed to control yourself"? excitedly said Michelle as they began to open up on a different level.

"I have not met anyone like you before, and to be honest, I'm terrified I might mess this up," said Xavier.

"You are a gentleman, and I think you are special. We're adults, and we can play a little," confessed Michelle.

Xavier felt his blood pressure increasing and felt the presence of his cock becoming hard while listing to Michelle's voice and comments. "You better be careful. The more I listen, things may get a little dirty," said Xavier.

Michelle thought for a second and conjured up the courage, "Okay, I'm listening, talk dirty to me."

Xavier laughed and said, "Are we serious?"

"Yes," said Michelle in a low, sexy tone.

Xavier thought for a second and asked, "What shirt do you have on at this moment?"

Michelle nervously considered her answer and almost spewed a lie but said, "To be honest, I am naked in my bed with only my black thigh-high pantyhose on. Is that okay with you?" asked Michelle.

"Wow, hum, well, I'm speechless. No, no, I think that is sexy," nervously replied Xavier. "In fact, I think that image is possibly the most exciting thing I have ever imaged," said Xavier.

"What are you wearing?" asked Michelle.

Xavier was nude and considered lying, but he was excited at Michelle's admittance and said, "Nothing."

Michelle bit her lip, felt a slight tingle within her pussy, and said, "You are making me excited."

Xavier became increasingly excited and confessed he called her because he had become too excited to sleep. After all, she caused a reaction within him that was sending him into a crazy state.

"What reaction are you're talking about?" asked Michelle.

"I think you know," said Xavier.

"Know what?" said Michelle.

"I am so into you that my cock is about to burst at the sound of your voice," said Xavier.

Michelle sat upright in her bed as she felt a warm rush of excitement pulse through her body and asked, "Will you grab your dick and tell me how it feels?" asked Michelle.

Xavier pulled the cover off his naked body and changed the phone to another ear while wrapping his fingers around his rock-hard dick and saying, "It's hard to the touch but soft and feels good to pull the skin up and down while listening to the sound of your sexy voice."

"Touch your balls," said Michelle.

"I'm jerking off at the moment and will gladly touch my balls, but first, I need to know what you're doing," said Xavier.

"My breast feels large and soft while my left hand rubs them gently," explained Michelle. "My right finger is wet and rubbing my pussy while I think of watching you stroke your manhood," said Michelle.

Xavier began to jerk his dick faster at the thought of Michelle nude and playing with her pussy.

"I can hear you're beating your shaft faster," said Michelle. "The sound of your body moving, and your increased breathing is making me wet," explained Michelle.

"I would lick your finger and bury my tongue deep in your body if I was there," stated Xavier.

"I can do better, and I would press your willing tongue into my pussy while I swallowed your hard dick at the same time," excitedly explained Michelle.

Xavier was filled with passion as he and Michelle masturbated together over the phone. As Michelle rubbed her clit faster and faster, she asked, "Would you cum in my mouth?"

"I would shoot every drop into your perfect mouth," admittedly replied Xavier as he felt his body pumping his balls full of cum as he approached his explosion.

"Fuck, I want you to fuck me with your hard dick," said Michelle.

Michelle could clearly overhear Xavier pumping his shaft as his breathing was off the chart. She then heard him moaning as she continued to let out passionate sighs of excitement and moans of pleasure.

"I want to hear you cum, Michelle," pleaded Xavier.

"Fuck, I'm close. My pussy is so wet and messy," said Michelle as she arched her back and vigorously rubbed her pussy.

Michelle felt her body tensing as she heard Xavier let out a loud moan. "Oh shit, I'm fucking coming. It just shot all over my chest," said Xavier.

Michelle, at this point, was about to explode while listening to Xavier moan and release his sounds of pleasure as he was shooting his load all over his body. She let out a scream as she felt all her sexual tension push out of her pussy while releasing her juices that spurted onto her sheets. She moaned and cursed as she moved her head back and forth as her pussy popped and released sounds of extreme wetness.

Michelle's body continued to pulse and release waves of pleasure as she overheard Xavier slowing his breathing. They both slowed their motions as their bodily fluids finished spilling out of their warm and stimulated bodies.

"You sound amazing, Michelle," said Xavier.

"You sounded pretty good yourself," said Michelle in a low, sexy tone that vibrated with small finishing pulses ringing out her pussy.

"My body is a mess. I have cum running down my balls, all over my belly, and some that splattered as far as my neck," explained Xavier.

Michelle felt an extreme amount of pleasure at the thought of her making Xavier cum. "You should see my fingers and how wet my sheets are at this moment," explained Michelle.

Xavier, at this point, was slowly rubbing his balls and pumping his dick as slow trickles of cum dripped onto his belly. He could only imagine sucking Michelle's cum from her fingers as he pushed his dick into her swollen, wet pussy. Michelle could not erase the image of Xavier's cum running down the back of his hand as she slowed the invasion of her erect clit.

"That was nice," said Michelle.

"That was awesome," replied Xavier.

As Xavier's blood returned to his brain, Xavier was a little embarrassed that Michelle witnessed his stimulated state. At the same time, Michelle began to wonder what all she said during their horny exchange.

"Can we do this again sometime?" asked Xavier.

"Good night, Xavier, and to answer your question, yes," said Michelle as he hung up the phone.

CHAPTER 15

Michelle and Xavier had been dating now for ten months; life was almost as perfect as it could be for them both. Michelle had developed a deep sense of attachment toward Xavier and continued each day with no disappointment of choosing to be with just Xavier and eliminating her promiscuous habits of the past. Xavier was ecstatic over Michelle and could barely focus each day while anticipating the time he will spend with her. Xavier had thought a lot about Michelle and how he wanted to ask her to be in his future forever but was afraid Michelle might think he was moving too fast. Michelle counted down the days and hours in anticipation of being with Xavier and had thought deeply about what life would be like if she and Xavier lived together. Michelle and Xavier have talked dirty, make out while masturbating together over the phone on several occasions. Masturbation from a distance had become an activity they both find intriguing and an event they find pleasing. Xavier and Michelle both felt a sense of youthfulness, carelessness, and the ability to have fun while working on their relationship. In contrast, both have practiced extreme discipline not to have sex physically when together.

Michelle sat at her desk and looked at a picture of her and Xavier together on top of a mountain in East Tennessee they climbed. Michelle held her phone out with her hand and snapped a selfie of her and Xavier kissing with a fantastic view in the background, revealing breathtaking mountains. She kissed her pointer and middle finger and touched Xavier in the pic while she began to examine her daily schedule. Michelle noticed the husband and wife she counseled was on her schedule for today and wondered what they had been up to over the past several months. The husband and wife canceled several of their last therapy sessions, but Michelle was hoping to see the couple and discover if they had made progress as a couple. The previous session involved just the wife stressing how she felt her husband was beginning to move away from the connection they have created and felt he did not desire their sexual encounters in a collaborative effort while making many trips to the private gatherings with his friend. She decided to ask her husband several months before to attend the newfound place with him.

"Michelle, your 9:00 a.m. appointment has arrived," stated Michelle's receptionist over the speakerphone.

"Please send them in," asked Michelle.

Michelle's door opened up, and she saw the couple's husband but not the wife. "Come on in, how have you been?" asked Michelle.

The husband looked bad and stressed and asked if he could please shut the door because his conversation was urgent and private.

Michelle agreed to a closed-door interaction only because of his urgency and asked, "What is wrong?"

Tears fell down his face as he looked at Michelle and expressed, "My wife is missing now for three days and has not returned my calls or text."

"Have you contacted the police?" asked Michelle with an urgent voice as she picked up the phone.

"No, stop, I have fucked up, and I need your help trying to find my wife," stressed the husband. "You are the only person I can reveal my outings with because of my position," said the husband. "I'm a state senator, as you know, and I cannot call the police because it would reveal my sexual history and destroy my standing with the state," cried out the husband.

"Okay, let's start from the beginning and see if we can figure out what has happened," said Michelle.

The husband's hands shook, and a deep sense of confusion poured out through his terrified expressions as he started to explain how his wife asked him several months prior if she could begin attending the private gatherings with him and his friend.

"I was happy she wanted to come along, so we set a date for her and me to attend with our friends," said the husband. "I was a bit afraid she would become angry to discover I had started to participate in sexual actions with other men without her presence," said the husband.

The husband began to reveal the details of their first visit within the private club and how he and his wife started to enjoy the presence of each other again. "I do love my wife, but I have discovered the presence of a man to be sexually stimulating while different than a woman, and if that information were released to the public, I would be scrutinized by many," said the husband.

"Let us try to focus on the details of your visits and try to set aside your political position for the moment," begged Michelle.

The husband continued to explain how he and his wife entered the club with their friends who provided the access. He explained how he noticed his wife becoming excited when she observed the number of people within the areas while engaging in sexual acts. As the husband and wife sat in the lounge area talking and consuming drinks, they decided to walk back to one of the rooms and have sex. They entered a darkened place and included streams of laser lights that moved over people's bodies while revealing them in various sexual acts. The wife had become stimulated and began kissing her husband and friend's wife while unzipping her husband's pants and sucking his cock with the other wife's participation.

"I had forgotten how I enjoyed watching my wife guide her friends head up and down my penis while I watched and soaked in the pleasures of their warm mouths."

As the two wives played with his dick and touched each other, the husband began to observe the other man sitting on the lap of another man while grabbing his dick from between his legs and guiding it into his ass. "I noticed my wife watching the men and how she knew I enjoyed the view," expressed the husband.

He continued to explain how she stood up as the other wife sucked hard on his cock and walked over to the two men and said something to them. He noticed she kissed the other man while playing with his dick as the man fucked him in the ass. She looked back at the husband and smiled as she bent over and started to suck the man's dick while he was riding the man's cock.

After several minutes of watching his wife enjoy the man's cock, he noticed the man was cumming in his friend's ass as the sight of the three entangled sexually sent him gushing cum deep into the other wife's mouth as she swallowed his load. As the man finished releasing his load into his friend's body, his wife walked over and kissed deeply with the woman who had a fresh load pumped into her mouth by her husband. She leaned forward and asked him to suck the husband's dick for her while she watched, for she knew through the other wife the two men were fucking on occasion. He was relieved she approved of his actions and eagerly began to desire the friend's cock in his mouth. The husband got on his knees and positioned his mouth over his friend's cock and began to fill his mouth with his length. He enjoyed the hard feeling of a dick sliding over his tongue while experiencing the taste of precum on occasions. As he twisted his mouth and sucked hard on his bulging dick, he would slide his tongue around the head of his dick, sending a tickling effect through his friend's body while he squeezed his large balls with his hand. His friend placed both hands on each side of his head as he screamed out with pleasure and pumped waves of thick cum into his mouth. The husband said he enjoyed the taste of his friend's cum and found his dick to be pleasing to play with and fuck on occasion.

The husband continued to explain how his wife became accepting of him and his sexuality with men while eventually encouraging and watched him fuck many other men within the club over several months. "Sex with another man became the normal practice of our encounters and often included my wife in the mix as well as we found a new way of enhancing our sexual encounters once again," explained the husband. "We begin to be like old times again. We would fuck many people in the club and then enjoy each other usually before we could make it back home," explained the husband.

"Our sexual connection was firing on all cylinders once again as we could not keep our hands off each other and looked forward to watching each other fuck many people," said the husband. "My wife would come by the office with nothing on but her long jacket and high heels and would fuck me on my desk while asking me to tell her how much I loved to suck and fuck other men," said the husband. "She even brought her friend over once who positioned herself under my desk and sucked my dick discreetly while several people came in and out of my office," explained the husband.

"Michelle, as you can see, my history is littered with details that my opponents would love to hold against me," eagerly explained the husband.

"What happened to your wife?" firmly asked Michelle.

"Sorry, I have talked too much," said the husband.

The husband shared the details of an event that involved him and his wife and the couple entering the private club one night after several visits while a man approached them and asked if he could have a word with them. He brought them to a room, sat them down, explained how they all knew who he was, and firmly demanded his silence and secrecy concerning the underground activities of the club. The man said he and the club organizers wanted to grant him and his wife access and membership exclusively to the restricted areas. The husband was excited to hear the news as this meant he could eventually show his wife the bull.

"Can my wife fuck the bull?" quickly asked the husband.

"Fuck the bull, what makes you think she can handle the bull?" asked the man.

"She can handle any dick you shove into her," said the husband.

"We'll see about that." Laughed the man.

The husband's wife did become excited to the mention of meeting the bull; she had heard much detail from her husband and had fantasied many times about taking his dick within her body.

The man walked around the couple and stopped at his wife. "You are gorgeous. Why would your husband want to share you with a wild animal like the bull?" said the man while glaring at her eyes and touching her long, blond hair.

The wife sat and listened to the attractive man compliment her beauty and became even more excited as he rubbed the back of his hand against her face and said, "I think the bull would enjoy making you scream."

The wife looked at the man and smirked a smile. "Okay, let's find out if the bull can handle me," joked the wife.

"Oh, in time, my lovely. You don't choose him, he chooses you," explained the man.

The man's phone rang on his desk, and he asked the couples to please excuse him as they exited the office. The wife laughed with the other woman and teased the guys about the bull being so scary. The men had experienced the bull up close and seen how massive he was and how hard he fucked his mates.

"I'm telling you, the guy we saw is no joke," expressed the husband.

The couples turned their heads back as they heard the man's voice asking the wife if she would please join him privately in the conversation for a moment within his office.

She looked back and smiled at her husband, saying, "Looks like I might have to tame the bull."

The husband told Michelle he was excited but also afraid concerning how hard the bull fucked the other woman while almost grabbing his wife by the arm and asking her to forget this request he had offered.

He explained that his wife walked into the office as the man shut the door, and after several minutes, his wife came back out and smiled as if she just won a special prize. She explained to the others how the man asked her to sit while he sat on the front of his desk positioned directly in front of her body. He explained how he just received a call stating she was approved to be part of the show and participating in a sexual encounter with the bull. He asked her to look at the camera mounted in the corner of the room and take off her clothing. She became nervous but wanted to do what it takes to be the leading woman. She stood up and pulled her sexy dress over her shoulders, allowing it to drop directly onto the floor while revealing her naked form.

"You have a nice body, he will be pleased to taste your flesh," explained the man. "The bull requires the complete submission. No part or opening is off-limits. He will fuck you as hard and in any way he wants," said the man. "If he wants your ass, then you will bend over. If he wants you to swallow, you will swallow. You will do whatever he wants for as long as he wants even if it involves twenty cocks. Get it?" asked the man.

The woman agreed and slipped her clothing back on while the man handed her a card with a date and time attached while exiting the office.

CHAPTER 16

The wife laughed as she regained the group and showed them the card the man had handed her with a bullhead image in the background colored black while containing a date and time.

"I told her the man was massive and had a huge cock, but she would not listen and counted the days down until she was going to fuck him," cried the husband.

The date arrived, and the husband explained how she had prepared all week with expensive hair coloring and body maintenance that looked fantastic. She had fucked the husband's dick many times over the last several days, and while fucking him, she continued over and over, talking about how she was going to put on a show for him.

"I liked how she talked dirty, and I wanted it just as much as she did," said the husband.

Michelle listened closely and wrote down many points of interest while the husband told her about the last night he saw his wife. He explained how she wore a white dress so low her cleavage would pop out if you hit a bump in the road and how eager they all were while anticipating the event. As they arrived, the man at the door took his wife's card and asked them to follow another person to a locker area. Like before, they all removed their clothing, placed all personal items within the lockers, and lined up behind many couples.

While in line, a man walked out, placed a flowered head ordainment onto his wife, and asked her to please follow him while they disappeared off into another doorway. "We all were excited and could not wait until we witnessed my wife pleasing the mammoth-sized man," explained the husband.

At this point, the friend's wife was directly behind her mate with her hand around his waist while her right hand reached behind and played with the husband's dick.

"I was excited and ready as the man explained the rules once again, and we walked into the dimly lightened arena and sat on the stadium-style seating while circling the wooden bench within the center of the area. I noticed my wife with her floral head ornament and wearing a rose-colored robe while on her knees with her hands directly at her side and looking downward," explained the husband.

"The environment was cool, but you could feel the heat of the torches surrounding the area now and then. A man entered the room and demanded everyone to their feet as two large wooden doors opened, revealing the silhouette of a large man with horns proceeding out of his head. As the man entered the light, his body was substantial and covered with various leather coverings while possessing a collar with two long ropes led by two other men. The horns on his head were large and dark-colored while his dick hangs long and swinging back and forth with his balls, smacking his legs from time to time. We were all ordered to sit as the beast walked closer to my wife," said the husband.

"I became terrified once again as he stretched out his massive arms and his muscles flexed while pushing all his veins to the surface of his skin. He released a devilish roar as he stared into the crowd and examined his guest. I caught the sight of my wife looking up at the beast with her eyes opened widely while she appeared to be breathing rapidly," explained the husband.

The two men who directed the bull walked over to the man's wife and pulled her to her feet while removing her rose-colored robe and revealing her nakedness as the bull approached her from the front and stood before her as if he were going to devour the flesh from her body. He licked his lips as if he approved of his delicious treat and rubbed his dick in a downward motion.

"I remember the look on my wife's face as if she was suddenly terrified as to what stood before her," expressed the husband in panic. The muscle-bound beast walked around the husband's wife while observing her well-rounded features and stood behind her. "I looked around the room as we all began to touch ourselves from the onset of what was about to happen," said the husband.

The horned man placed his hands on the wife's shoulders and began to run his forked tongue up and down her soft neck. The wife, at this point, reached up and placed her hand on the beast's hand and gave into the touch of his approach. She laid her head back as his hands found their way to her firm breasts, and he continued to suck and bite on her neck area. The wife began to bit her lips as her eyes rolled back in pleasure as he softly caressed her body and tasted her flesh. She moaned as he rubbed her pussy opening while pressing his long dick against her bare ass. The beast pulled her hair with an aggressive motion as he sank his fang-shaped teeth into the wife's shoulder area, causing her to let out a subtle scream as a small amount of blood rolled down her back. He ran his tongue through her blood trail and licked his lips as he pulled away and lay on the wooden bench while pulling the willing wife toward him.

She climbed up on the table while grabbing his long meat with her right hand and dragging her wet tongue across his exposed stomach muscles. The bull pulled her body around and positioned her in a 69 position while sinking his mouth onto her wet pussy.

The wife moaned as the beast sucked and licked her horny pussy while she lowered her head and stretched her mouth wide, trying to take in his thick girth. As she sucked his large cock head, she moaned loudly as he slurped up her juices and licked her clit aggressively. She pushed her hips deep onto his mouth as she placed much effort into taking his length into her mouth. The beast pushed his hips upward, causing the wife to gag loudly as his hard dick penetrated her throat. The wife turned her head and found her husband, who was stroking his meat quickly as he caught sight of spit streaming from the beast's cock to his wife's mouth. Her eyes bleed strips of black mascara as her eyes watered from the extensive gagging as he thrusted his meat deep into her mouth. His hands stretched open her ass cheeks as he enjoyed the moisture flowing out of her dripping pussy.

The wife felt her body tightening as the bull licked up and down her erect clit and found his large balls to suck up into her mouth as she prepared to cum. She held tight to his dick with her right hand as she squeezed her eyes shut with her head downward and let out a screaming sound as she released her well into the depths of his mouth. She twisted her hips, trying to redirect the tickling effect, but the strength of the beast did not allow her to control her fate as her body pulsed with waves of orgasms while screaming. She almost passed out as the beast will not allow her a moment to recover as her body dumped waves of pussy cum over his wondering tongue. She laid her moaning head onto his leg as she continued to pump his long meat with her hand as she whimpered and shook uncontrollably.

"I exploded at the sight of my wife ejaculating on the beast's mouth while sucking his dick," explained the husband. "As I came, my friend leaned over and took my remaining waves of cum into his mouth, sending me into sexual bliss as his wife's legs were spread wide, playing with her pussy and enjoying the entertainment," said the husband. "I held onto my friend's head as he sucked me dry and observed the bull standing and demanding my wife to stand at the foot of the wooden table," explained the husband.

The bull became more aggressive as he violently pulled the wife's hairs and pushed her head to the wooden table while pulling her ass out toward his cock. He took his hands and dragged her legs open more expansive and rubbed his dick into the wetness of her pussy. She moaned loudly as he pushed his massive dick into her wet pussy.

"I could hear the sounds of her pussy popping from the excessive wetness as he started to fuck her deeply," said the husband.

The wife's body jerked aggressively as the beast fucked her harder than any man has ever achieved and caused her to drip excessively onto the wooden table. Suddenly, the bull pulled his shiny, wet dick out of the wife and pressed it into the opening of her ass, causing her to scream out in intense pain due to the intrusion of his massive size.

"I lost myself within the moment as I became overly excited. I should have tried to stop him, but somehow, I liked watching him brutally fucking my wife's tight ass," confessed the husband.

During this time, the friend's wife had spread open with her back toward the husband and slid her wet pussy onto his horny dick and began to move her lovely ass up and down his dick. "It all felt so good, and watching my wife's firm tits shaking as her ass was invaded was pleasing while my dick enjoyed my friend's wet pussy," said the husband.

The husband's wife cried out in pain as the bull rammed his dick deep into her ass over and over while his hanging balls smacked hard against her pussy fold. The bull pulled her hair hard again and caused more pain by pressing his teeth into her back area, causing her to bleed rapidly. The wife pleaded for the bull to stop and reached out to her husband, who ignored her call and enjoyed the friend riding his hard dick. Tears fell from her face as her mouth spewed out strings of spit as blood dripped from her back onto the table. The bull grabbed her hips more brutally as he increased his depth and speed, sending the wife into extreme pain while he arched his back and laid his head back and powered a massive shot of cum into the depths of her ass. He pushed his dick deeper into her body, with every wave of cum spewing out of his pulsing cock until he released every drop.

The bull kept his dick deep in her ass as she cried while assuring every drop remained in her ass as he observed the guests' pleasure of the night's events. The husband was sidelined with sexual energy as the friend's wife continued to move her ass over his dick and let him release his second load inside her wet pussy. As the husband ejaculated in her pussy, he pulled her back up against his chest while fondling her small breast as he finished. While the friend's wife slowly pumped his dick, the husband observed the bull's meat slide out of his wife's ass and hung with a great length which sent a tickling effect throughout his body.

"He fucking took her! He took her away!" shouted the husband.

"Wait, please slow down and tell what happened. What do you mean he took her?" asked Michelle.

The man explained that as he and the other wife finished fucking, he saw the bull grab his wife around the waist and carried her off to the large wooden doors. He had not seen or heard from her in three days.

"I thought we would meet back up in the dressing room, but when we were dressed and lead out another door, she was still not there. We were told to keep our mouths shut if we knew what was best and sent out another door that was an exit you could not reenter," explained the man.

The husband continued to explain how he had tried for three days to enter the private club, but they will not let him back in and told him never to return.

"I'm fucked, I do not know what to do, and you're the only person I can talk to who will not judge me," cried the husband. "I have messed up. I want her back. Will you please help me, Michelle? I will give you anything you want. I have plenty of money. Name the price," said the husband.

"Okay, there has to be a reason why she has not returned," said Michelle. "Do you think she may have stayed by her own will?" asked Michelle.

"I don't know. What do I do?" asked the husband. "I tried to pay the bouncer at the door, he would not listen. I asked to see the man in charge, they denied me. I think she may be in trouble," said the husband.

"Do you think she is in trouble, or are you just afraid this will expose your political career?" directly asked Michelle.

"Fuck you, I love my wife. Who do you think you are judging me!" screamed the husband.

Michelle became silent for a moment and apologized for her comment but knew down inside he was covering his tracks due to the negative effect it would cause if the local authorities were to investigate the missing person. Michelle thought for a moment and asked the husband if his friend would agree to pretend she was his date and try to get her into the private club.

"Thank you, thank you, I knew you would help. I will call him immediately and see if he will help," said the husband.

103

CHAPTER 17

Michelle thought long and hard, considering her next move and how to extract information once she gained an inside point of view. The situation was complicated, and she pondered whether she should withhold the information from the police. She had considered the idea of speaking with Xavier and asking what he would do, but her patient confidentiality was still in effect and must be protected. Michelle finished up her day and headed home. Once she reached her sofa, she dropped everything and fell back with her eyes closed while feeling nervous and fearful concerning helping the husband. Michelle picked up her phone from the onset of a text alert and saw it was from Xavier. Xavier made her happy, and she smiled big while she sat up to see what the message reads.

"Hey, hottie, are you free tomorrow night for a hot date with this guy?" asked Xavier.

Michelle, at this moment, did not have plans and was excited to spend more time with Xavier and quickly texted she would love a date tomorrow.

"Great, I want to take you over to Kingston for a nice dinner at the Charleston Bayside restaurant," explained Xavier.

Michelle's eyes became more prominent, and she knew the restaurant was a high-end establishment and responded "That sounds yummy. I'll be waiting" and ended with an emoji of a winking face.

"Looking forward to seeing that beautiful smile. I will pick you up at six thirty sharp," said Xavier.

Michelle kicked off her high heels and pulled off her dress, allowing it to settle on her living room floor while heading back toward her shower. She could not wipe off her smile if you slapped her at this moment and was overly excited to see her man again. Michelle turned on her hot water within her bathtub, poured in the bubbles, and anticipated the warmth and softness of the bubbles soaking into her skin. She popped the back of her bra and pulled down her panties, revealing her heart-shaped hair above her vagina. She placed her phone and played some soft classical music next to her tub and sank into the pleasurable water while closing her eyes and laying her head back to drown out the day's troubles. She rubbed her body with soaps and moved with the rhythm of the music as her phone sounded off with a FaceTime call.

Michelle quickly pulled her wet hair back while pushing the bubbles up around her ample breast. Michelle answered the phone with excitement, "Hello, Xavier."

Xavier looked confused and said, "Oh, I'm sorry, I did not mean to bother you while you bathed."

"It's okay, cutie. What can I do for you?" said Michelle in a sexy tone.

"Now that's the million-dollar question that has a lot of openings I could fill in," said Xavier. "You look amazing, Michelle," said Xavier.

Michelle noticed Xavier pulling off his shirt and looked a bit sweaty. "What have you been up to?" asked Michelle.

"I have been moving some livestock for my father and had to restock several rows of straw," stated Xavier.

"You mean the straw we rolled around in the first night we met?" said Michelle as she provided Xavier with her trademark crooked smile.

"It was fun, but that bathtub filled with bubbles, and you look amazing," said Xavier.

Michelle blushed as she would give anything to pull Xavier into the bathtub with her and allow him to have his way with her body.

"Wow, lucky bubbles covering that amazing body," stated Xavier.

"Amazing body. Are you saying you like what I have, Xavier, you naughty boy?" said Michelle in an extreme lustrous voice.

"I do and think you are the hottest women I have ever met," said Xavier with a serious glare into the phone. "I love everything about you, Michelle, and I want to thank you tomorrow night for making me the happiest person in the world by doing something special," explained Xavier.

"And what might that be?" said Michelle as she leaned forward with a minimal number of bubbles covering her big breasts. Michelle provided Xavier much to stare at while trying to control his temptation to ask her to remove the bubbles.

"I look forward to tomorrow and hope you and your sexy body sleeps well. I needed to see that beautiful face before I went to sleep," said Xavier.

Michelle smiled and said, "Good night, I'll see you tomorrow."

*****

Xavier's alarm clock sounded. He rolled over to slap the off button while rubbing his eyes and letting out a big yawn. He grabbed his phone to find a picture Michelle sent him of her laying in her bed while the camera caught the position of her body from the midsection of her cleavage up to her face.

Xavier said out loud, "Fuck, I want to see what's below that camera."

Michelle was the queen of sending sexy pics that left little to the imagination but enough censorship to leave you gnawing at the bit to see more. *I'll get her and her flirting game*, thought Xavier.

Xavier ran into the kitchen, grabbed a banana, and lay on his bed while holding the camera upward; he slipped the banana in his underwear, making it seem like he had a firm erection while holding onto the outside of his underwear. He pushed the record button and filmed himself, saying "Hey, Michelle, what do you think of this?" as he rolled the camera down his chest, belly, and then over his banana bulge that appeared to be a large hard cock protruding under his underwear while clicking send to Michelle.

Xavier became excited and laughed out loud as he anticipated what Michelle would think when she viewed his video. He felt a rush of nervousness came over him as he heard his phone chime with a response from Michelle reading "You have my utmost attention" while including an emoji with devil horns.

Xavier paused for several seconds and tried to think of the best way to respond to the queen of flirting. He pulled his phone upward and clicked record as the phone panned over his chest, belly, and once again revealing a bulge in his underwear; he pulled out the banana and peeled it back while staring into the camera and took a big bite and winked at Michelle.

Michelle observed the video and thought *Oh no, you didn't just do that, you are a fucking tease, I cannot lose at this game* while laughing and conjuring up a perfect response. Michelle pulled off her shirt and positioned her camera on her night table while turning her back toward the camera and placing her hands directly on her bed backboard while naked with her ass covered only with a sheet while looking back at her phone.

"Hey, Siri, record a video," stated Michelle.

Xavier's phone chimed while he eagerly anticipated her response and opened the video to see how Michelle responded. The footage made Xavier sit upright with urgency, revealing Michelle's naked back in a knelt position with her ass covered only with a sheet. Her brunette hair hangs down her sexy golden-colored back while she appeared to be touching herself between her legs. Xavier lusted for more and wanted desperately for Michelle to turn around and reveal herself to him.

Michelle's movement stopped as she turned her head and smiled at the camera, saying "I just love beating off my eggs early in the morning" as she moved a bowl of eggs with an eggbeater into the camera frame. She winked at the camera and said, "Xavier, nice try. I will always win this game. Siri, stop recording."

Xavier bent his head back and rubbed his face while he felt a massive surge of excitement as he caught the sight of Michelle's back and her sexy curves. He smiled noticeably big and rewound the camera to pause on Michelle as she looked from the side, smiling and revealing a small portion of her side boob and exposed back. Xavier was looking at the most beautiful person he had ever seen while his dick became so hard it almost hurt from the sudden rush of sexual desire flowing through his body.

Xavier texted Michelle and said, "Okay, yes, you won." And without thinking, he wrote, "I just love you so much." He excitedly sent the text. He laughed again and realized he sent "I love you" to Michelle and beginning to feel a little bit of panic.

Silence swept over the moment for several seconds, which felt like an eternity to Xavier as he started to write back "Sorry, I didn't mean love as in love, love" while stopping and thinking, *I do love her, I love her*. He deleted the last text without sending. Xavier saw his text read, "read," while becoming nervous about how Michelle would respond. Xavier could not see Michelle's physical reaction, but she looked at the text with her hand over her mouth as tears began to fall from her face. Michelle discovered she loved Xavier several months prior but has not dared to admit it personally to Xavier.

Xavier's phone alerted a reply that read, "I love you too, Xavier." Xavier thought for a second and grabbed his phone, saying "Not like this" while FaceTiming Michelle.

As the phone connected, Xavier saw Michelle had been crying and quickly said, "I said it, and I do love you, Michelle."

Xavier continued to say, "I have loved you for a time, and it slipped out because it's just there and needed to be let out," he stuttered and nervously explained. "I desire you, I love you, and never want to be apart from you," firmly stated Xavier.

Michelle looked at Xavier and smiled. "You just gave the perfect start to my day. I do love you and thankful to be part of your life," said Michelle as she cleaned the tears from her eyes.

Xavier smiled and took a big breath, and said, "I did not know how you would respond, and those few seconds seemed like an eternity."

Michelle leaned forward to the phone and gave Xavier a big screen kiss and said, "I love you, mister, let's pick up tonight where we left off this morning."

Xavier smiled big and said, "Tonight will be special. I'll be waiting for you at six thirty tonight."

Michelle and Xavier hung up the phones and began their day in a direction they had not experienced within their lives.

CHAPTER 18

Michelle walked into her office area with a glow of happiness that everyone noticed. "Michelle, you look as if you just won a million dollars," said Michelle's secretary.

Michelle smiled and said, "No, life is just good today."

Michelle's secretary replied with a smile and said, "I know that look. It's Xavier, right?"

Michelle looked at her longtime employee and said, "My office in five."

After a few minutes passed, Michelle's secretary walked in, sat down, and said, "Okay, what happened? Did you and Xavier do it?"

Michelle giggled and said, "No, we did not have sex. He told me he loved me."

Michelle's secretary's mouth fell wide open and said, "Well, what did you say back?"

Michelle opened her eyes wide and loudly said, "I told him I love him too."

Michelle's secretary giggled like a teen and said, "It's time to give him that booty, Michelle."

Michelle laughed out loud as she knew the statement was true and contained her deepest desire. Michelle's secretary stood up to return to her desk as the phone was ringing and buzzing. Michelle's secretary asked if she could take an urgent call.

Michelle answered in haste and discovered a familiar voice. "Michelle, I hired one of my closet friends to research my wife's whereabouts, and they said an anonymous source told them she was within the complex," stated her client.

Michelle asked the senator, "Do you think she has stayed on her own free will?"

The senator responded, "No, I was told she is being kept in some fucking dungeon below the complex and looks like she has been beaten."

Michelle placed her hand on her forehead and pondered the information and said, "Why would they be holding her against her will?"

The senator responded, "It's got to be for fucking political gain or blackmail. We have to get her out of there somehow." The senator continued to say, "I'm taking some muscle with me, and I'm going up there this afternoon and demanding the release of my wife."

Michelle told the senator to be careful and urged him to call the police once more.

The husband responded, "I'm going to take care of this once and for all. They do not know who they are fucking with."

Michelle urged the senator to call her once he found out any information concerning his wife. Michelle felt a sense of relief concerning the whereabouts of the senator's wife and hoped the issue would be resolved quickly. She thought about the mess the couple's sexual journey had caused and wondered how this would end without the authorities knowing about the crime.

Michelle accepted her following clients' time slot and tried to focus on their troubles while drifting in and out concerning the senator's dilemma. Michelle listened to her client explain how she has a problem with convincing her lover to leave his wife. When she was young, the client explained how she lived next door to an attractive man who would regularly invite her and her family over for a cookout and pool party. Her bedroom window was positioned directly across from the neighbor's master bedroom, where she would discreetly view the couple having sex regularly late at night. Michelle discovered the woman would become excited when describing the couple fucking as she watched and touched her body. She explained how she became obsessed with the husband. She started walking around her room at night naked with all the lights on when she saw him in his room, or she would lay out back in the sun with her clothing off due to his office window possessing a view that could see directly into her fenced-in backyard area. The woman stated she wanted to be the woman he was married to and made great efforts to make him notice her.

The woman described how the families were attending another pool party at their home, and when people started to leave, she asked if she could stay behind and swim a bit longer. While the neighbors said it would be okay, she described how she watched the wife clean up and headed into the house while the husband stayed behind and straightened up the area. The husband walked over to her and made small talk while sitting on the side of the pool with his legs in the water.

"You know, you should try closing your curtains. You can see into your room," stated the husband.

"You might want to close your curtains, especially when it's late at night," said the woman as she smiled at the man.

The man looked over his shoulder as his wife yelled out that she was going upstairs to take a shower. The woman said she looked at the man and asked him if he wanted to join her for a swim.

"Uh, I don't think that would be a good idea," stated the husband.

"What's not a good idea concerning swimming in a pool with a woman? It's your pool," said the young girl.

The man stared at her pretty face and slipped into the water. The girl moved close to the man and remained quiet as she removed her top.

"Wait, we can't do this. You're my friend's daughter, and I'm married," said the husband.

The woman explained how she placed her fingers on his lips and said, "Be quiet, no one will never know. It's okay, it's just sex."

The husband pulled her legs up around his body and pressed his mouth hard onto hers as they released built-up tension from observing each other over many occasions. The woman described how she wanted to be his and only his and have all the babies he could pump into her body. Michelle looked puzzled at the woman and knew she had severe psychological issues. The woman looked like she was in complete pleasure as she described how he pulled open her bathing suit bottom and slid his long dick deep in her pussy and aggressively fucked her hard up against the side of the pool for several minutes as he shot his load in her pussy.

"He fucked me so good, and as he finished his cum and was kissing me, his wife yelled out for him. He tried to pull me away, but I held on tight because I wanted her to fucking know he wanted my pussy more than hers," stated the woman. "He got out of the pool in just enough time to wrap a towel around him and head off into the house. I lay back and felt his cum tingling inside my wet pussy, and it was wonderful," excitedly explained the woman.

"How long have you and the man been having an affair?" asked Michelle.

"I wouldn't call it an affair. It's a relationship, and I have fucked him for the last four years," said the woman. "We love each other and take advantage of every moment we can. I even fucked him on his sofa when his wife was getting ready for their date night while I was babysitting their two-year-old, and I once stayed over for the night watching their child and woke him up to suck his dick on their bedroom floor as his wife slept," spitefully explained the woman.

Michelle felt a rush of guilt, for it reminded her of what she did with Carl, her friend's husband, on the sofa. "Has your lover expressed any indications that he loves you and is going to leave his wife?" asked Michelle.

"Oh yes, just a few months ago while we met late at night outside and fucking in his car, he told me as he was inside me that he loved me," stated the woman.

"I think when people are entangled in a sexual experience, they say things that enhance the moment but necessarily may not be the most accurate information," explained Michelle. "Has he told you directly that he is going to leave his wife for you?" asked Michelle.

"No, he won't fucking leave her. I have threatened to expose our relationship if he stops fucking me," explained the woman.

"So why are you here with me?" asked Michelle.

"I cannot stop fucking him. I tried for a month but could not make myself stop. I'm here because when I fuck him, all I can do is think about how I want his wife to disappear," explained the woman. "Do I tell the wife about us so we can be together, or do I continue to fuck him until he decides I'm the better woman?" asked the woman.

Michelle looked at the woman and said, "You are confused and living a life of fantasy with an obsession for another woman's husband." She looked at the woman straight in her eyes and said, "He is not going to leave his wife. You are his pastime and sex relief, and the only reason he has continued is because you blackmailed him. He is never going to take you as his wife."

The woman jumped up and screamed at Michelle, "You fucking bitch, you will see. He loves me, and I will have him. You are no different than all the other therapists who told me the same thing." The woman stormed out the door as Michelle was left sitting in awe of what she just observed while her secretary looked in with a startled gaze and informed her she had another urgent call waiting.

Michelle answered the phone and realized it was the senator once again. Michelle leaned forward and slumped her head on her hand as she listened to his request.

"Michelle, thank you for taking my call. This is all fucked up and continues to escalate while getting worse," expressed the senator.

"What do you mean, Senator?" asked Michelle.

The senator explained he took a good friend he trusts with him whom he had used as a bodyguard for many years and demanded the doorkeeper to let him see who was in charge or he would contact the police. The doorkeeper made a call and asked them to wait. The door came open, and the senator said "That's what I fucking thought" while leading to a room within the building. He described how he and his bodyguard were asked to sit in a couple of chairs within an office space.

A man walked into the room as the senator screamed, "Do you know who I fucking am? On the contrary, do know who you are fucking with?"

"I would advise you to sit the fuck down and close your mouth," aggressively said the man as about ten large men surrounded the senator.

"First, your wife agreed to meet the bull and accepted all the consequences!" shouted the man. Then suddenly, one of the men pulled a knife and placed it directly onto the senator's throat. "Second, do not come into my place acting like you have power. You have no control here," said the man.

The senator then witnessed the men pulling his bodyguard to the ground and hitting him over and over with their fists as they beat his face into an almost unrecognizable state. "Okay, please stop. I will pay you whatever you want. I need my wife back, please," pleaded the senator.

The man got close to the senator's face and said, "Oh, your wife will pay. She's paying with her ass, and there's not a fucking thing you can do about it because I have a little surprise, motherfucker." The man turned and pointed a remote to the TV, revealing a video feed that showed the senator's wife tied up while another man was fucking her doggy style over the side of a table while she was gagged with a silence ball.

"What the fuck is that going to do? It's a video of my wife fucking, so what, you prick!" screamed the senator.

The man backhanded the senator very hard while busting his lip and said "The video feed of your wife is for you, dumbass, but this video is for us" as the man changed the video feed. The feed revealed several videos of the senator engaging in sexual acts in the club, partaking in drug use, and participating in torturing women.

"Now, who is in fucking charge?" laughed the man.

"Please don't do this," pleaded the senator.

"Here's what is going to happen. You are going to report your wife is missing after you remove a large amount of her clothing to make it appear she has left you, then your wife is going to stay here for our pleasure, and then your mouth will stay fucking shut and only open when we need you to take care of our request," explained the man. "Don't worry about your cute little wife, she will be fucked by many men just like she wanted while bringing a great price for men who want to fuck a senator's wife," said the man.

The man turned the feedback to the senator's wife as he unmuted the TV that revealed her screaming as men took turns ramming their cocks deep into her ass. "See, she's having a great time, so get the fuck out of my face and do as your told, or the videos will drop to every news feed in the state while your career will be fucked!" shouted the man.

Michelle listened and felt sorry for the husband but knew he and his wife did this to themselves, but with compassion, she feared if she did not help, the wife who she cared for would be killed. Michelle said, "What can I do to help?"

The senator explained his friend with who he engaged with sexual acts within the club will get her access and asked if Michelle would meet with him and see if she could discover a way to get his wife out. "If you could just help me figure out how to get access to her, I can arrange a way for someone to get her out, and when we do, I will go to the police and reveal what I have done," stated the senator. "Please I know I have fucked up, I need your help. I know this could be dangerous, but I feel confident you could gain the information I would need to rescue her," asked the senator.

"I will do this one time and one time only because I care for you and your wife's safety and desperately want to get her out of this mess," said Michelle in a desperate voice.

"Thank you. My friend will text you for your address and will let you know when he will pick you up," said the senator.

CHAPTER 19

What have I gotten myself into? thought Michelle as she was finishing up her day and heading home to prepare for an evening with Xavier. Michelle tried to clear her mind while taking a deep breath as she unlocked the door to her apartment. She walked in and sat at her table for a few minutes and pondered if she should seek the advice of Xavier.

Should I just tell, or should I go once and see if I could help? thought Michelle. Michelle had grown to like the senator and his wife over the last several years speaking with them during counseling, and even though she did not agree with everything they have done, she liked them as people.

I have to try, and when I'm done trying, then I will know that I did all I could do to try and save her. This is my decision thought Michelle. She stood up and decided to make the best night she could and dress very sexy for her man, Xavier. Michelle reached into her closet and grabbed her dark-blue dress that would pull over her breast while exposing an opening down to just about her belly button. The length of the dress was short and complimented her silver heels with a matching purse.

"Perfect," said Michelle as she held the dress up to her front while modeling in the mirror.

Michelle took extraordinary measures to manicure her hair, nails, and makeup features. She pulled out her dark-red lipstick while splashing her body with her favorite perfume. She looked at the clock and said "Oh, shit, Xavier will be here in forty-five minutes" while slipping her dress over her exposed breasts and white-colored thigh-high pantyhose.

Michelle looked at the white panties and decided "Not tonight, this is going to be the night" as she threw her panties back in the drawer while going commando. She pulled out her earring collection and decided to wear silver loops while inserting a diamond stud into the side of her nose. Michelle fluffed her hair while running her hands down her dress and looked into the mirror, saying, "You are one hot and horny bitch, Michelle."

Michelle's phone rang, and as she went to answer, she paused and did not recognize the number while silencing the call. Her phone rang again as she saw it was the same number and answered, "Hello."

An unfamiliar voice said, "Michelle, this is the senator's friend, Jordan. Can I pick you up in a few minutes?" said Jordan with much anticipation.

"Now, tonight? I was about to walk out the door," said Michelle.

"Please, Michelle, this is our shot. I have arranged for us to have access to the private club tonight. This may be our only chance at getting back in before they associate me with the senator and bar me from entering," said Jordan.

Michelle threw her shiny purse onto her bed and disappointedly said, "I understand, I'll be waiting."

Michelle knew she might not have another shot at helping the senator and his wife and decided to break off her evening with Xavier. She sent Xavier a text stating, "Xavier, I'm so sorry but have to cancel our date tonight due to a situation with work. I love you and again sorry."

Xavier was already on his way to pick up Michelle and was saddened that Michelle had to cancel but understood while texting, "Hey, cutie, it's okay, we have plenty of time. How about a rain check?"

Michelle texted back, "You're the best. I'll make it up to you, promise."

Xavier replied, "No problem, I get it, work is work, and sometimes, it's an inconvenience."

Xavier was a couple of minutes out from Michelle's apartment but wanted to go ahead and leave the flowers he purchased her at her door as a surprise for when she returned home. Xavier parked across the street due to a lack of parking and stepped out with the flowers as he headed to Michelle's apartment. Xavier stopped as he observed a long black car stopped at the entrance to Michelle's apartment while Michelle walked out and hugged a man and got into the car.

Xavier was confused and decided to follow the car briefly as he was curious about her intentions. *Maybe, this is a work event, and she knows the person*, thought Xavier optimistically concerning Michelle. Xavier hesitated for a second and thought he would be out of line while following Michelle with curiosity about her whereabouts but decided he must know.

Meanwhile, Michelle and Jordan spoke intensely concerning their plan. "Michelle, I'm going to get you in the club, and then I'm going to exit quickly outside and wait across the street so no one will suspect or realize who I am," stated Jordan.

"Am I in danger?" Michelle asked firmly.

"Just go in and make your way to the lounge where you will find many people and order a couple of drinks while trying to extract any useful information," stated Jordan.

"Okay, but I need to know who you are," said Michelle.

"The truth, my wife and I are the senator's lovers, and I'm also involved within governmental duties," nervously stated Jordan.

"So you all are using me as a guinea pig to do your risky work!" shouted Michelle as she became more frustrated with the task.

Jordan gently placed his hand on Michelle's and said, "I need your help to get the senator's wife back. I will confess to you, the senator and I have done things that will ruin our lives if exposed. Please we got in too deep while playing out our fantasies, and now we're screwed, you are beautiful and our only option. You should not have a problem assimilating," pleaded Jordan.

Michelle turned her head and looked out the window for a few seconds and responded to Jordan. "Look, I'm already knee-deep in this thing, I will help, but you have to understand that I'm terrified that something may happen to me as well," explained Michelle.

"My wife and I have attended this club for many years and have established a certain status that allowed us to enter different areas of the club. Nothing till now has happened like this," explained Jordan.

"Keep explaining, please," firmly stated Michelle.

Jordan continued to explain how he and his wife reached a sexual peak and wanted more. One of his companions told him about the club and invited him to attend. "You have to have a special invite and escorted by a member to enter the club. This is why you must go with me," said Jordan.

"I have heard many things about what happens in the club from the senator and his wife. I cannot fuck someone to gain information. I have a wonderful man that I have established a relationship with, and he has changed my life. I am terrified as to what I'm about to witness," nervously explained Michelle.

"Keep to the lounge areas and special view rooms. Do not ask or accept to be part of private activities. That is where we all messed up," stressed Jordan.

The car pulled up to a dimly lit alley. Jordan leaned over to Michelle and asked, "Are you ready? Take a deep breath and put on a flirty approach, and you'll fit right in. As soon as you're in, I will pretend to take a call and ask to step outside. Please be careful," said Jordan.

"Okay, let's do this," said Michelle as she perked herself up and put on her sexy approach.

Jordan walked up to a door and held a card up to the window. The door opened to reveal a doorkeeper who welcomed Jordan and Michelle.

"Who is this lovely lad?" asked the doorkeeper.

"She is my evening treat if you get my drift," stated Jordan.

The doorkeeper smiled and said, "I won't keep you waiting for any longer, Jordan. Enjoy her."

Michelle followed Jordan into the building while cutting her flirtatious eyes at the doorman as he lustfully looked up and down

Michelle's unique features. The doorman watched Michelle's ass twist as she started to disappear down the darkened hall.

Michelle swallowed deeply and whispered to Jordan, "Where are we going?"

Jordan turned around and grabbed Michelle by the waist and whispered in her ear, "Watch what you say. There are ears and cameras everywhere." Jordan kissed Michelle on her cheek, pretended to view his phone as if he was taking a call, and walked back toward the entrance.

Michelle felt an overwhelming presence of fear, abandonment, and uncertainty as she started to descend further down the hall. She could overhear a faint sound of music in the distance as her heels clicked across the hard floor. The air possessed an odor of alcohol and smoke while passing people lined up in darkened areas of the hall talking. Michelle caught sight of a doorway just ahead, and as she approached, she saw a woman topless on her knees performing a blow job on a man who was holding a glass in one hand and guiding her head with the other. She could hear the sucking sounds and moans displaying from the couple's naughty actions as she passed. The man smiled and moved the woman's head faster as he caught sight of Michelle's beauty and reached out with his hand, extending his fingers to touch her as she passed. The music became louder as a couple opened the door to what appeared to be the lounge area while Michelle moved past to enter. Michelle felt a little more at ease once she entered the large room and caught sight of the bar area while observing couples mingling.

Michelle moved quickly to establish a seat at the bar area and ordered a Scotch and gin on the rocks. She downed the drink quickly without hesitation and asked for another. Michelle turned a bit to gain a better view of the room and discovered that an array of activities was happening within the room. People were talking, some laughing, while others appeared to be mad at each other. Some were alone, and others were in larger groups. She also noticed men with men and women with women while some groups contained one woman and many men. Cocktail girls floated around the bar with only heels and thongs while bearing their naked breasts. The bartender was a large, muscled man with only tight, black shorts with boots and a bow tie while his cock hung out in a leather-style pouch. Michelle noticed many people were making out and even caught sight of people jacking others off or giving oral sex from under the table. Some of the activities became visually stimulating while Michelle had to focus and stick to the task.

Women and men would leave in groups and exit out doorways on the other side of the lounge while some would be escorted to other areas by what appeared to be staff. Michelle thought about how she would be able to snoop around and needed some interaction to help gain information. A man approached Michelle, sat next to her at the bar, and asked if he could buy her a drink.

Not interested, but this is a start, thought Michelle as she agreed for him to buy her a drink.

"I haven't seen you here before. You are gorgeous. My name is Lester," stated the man.

Michelle could not resist the temptation to say, "Lester as in Lester the molester."

The man took a drink and laughed. "I get that all the time, especially from women."

Michelle laughed and said, "I'm sorry, it just slipped out. My name is Michelle."

The man stood up, extended his hand, and said "Nice to meet you, Michelle" as he sat back at the bar. "First time here, Michelle?" asked the man as he took a sip of his drink and caught sight of Michelle's cleavage.

"Yes, I'm here with a friend who seems to have slipped off somewhere," stated Michelle.

"That will happen a lot here. There is just about anything and everything you could desire behind many doors throughout," explained the man. "I was walking through and could not believe such a beautiful woman was left unattended. If you were mine, I would never leave your side," firmly stated the man as she touched Michelle's arm while barely hanging onto the counter from the excessive amounts of drinks he seemed to have consumed.

"Where is your date?" asked Michelle.

"No date tonight, but I would love to show you around and get to know you better," stated the man in a forward approach.

Michelle wanted nothing more than to tell Lester to fuck off but knew she had to gain access to the other areas somehow. "So, Lester, how long have you been attending the club?" asked Michelle as she turned and laid her hand on his leg while giving Lester much more to observe from the position of her body.

"Damn girl, you are the hottest piece of ass I have ever seen, and believe me, I have seen a lot of asses in here," said the man.

"I notice you have a blue-colored badge while others have different-ent colors. What do these badges mean?" said Michelle as she reached out with a flirtatious look and touched his badge.

Lester placed his hand on the inside portion of Michelle's leg. "Honey, this badge gets you into any room you see down here with the ability to make your wildest fantasies come true," explained Lester.

Michelle moved Lester's hand upon the top of her leg, trying to divert Lester's obvious intentions of finding his way to her pussy.

"I have attended this club for a couple of years and earned the blue title. I'm in the hope of earning the black badge," said Lester.

"What's a black badge get you?" asked Michelle.

Lester moved close to Michelle's ear and said, "Sexual pleasure beyond your craziest dreams. I have also heard some people have earned a gold badge which gets you to access to the lower levels."

Michelle remembered Jordan flashed a gold badge upon entering the club and knew she needed to ditch Lester and find someone with a higher status.

Lester grabbed Michelle by the hand and said, "Here, let me show you what's behind the doors with my access," stated Lester.

Michelle stood up and followed Lester as he led her by his hand; he approached a door where a man looked at his badge and allowed them to enter.

CHAPTER 20

Michelle stepped through the guarded doorway as she followed Lester while nervousness sank deep into her belly. She observed a hallway with many doors. As they approached the first doorway, Lester turned and grabbed Michelle by the hips and asked, "What are you into, baby?"

Michelle swallowed her nervous energy and blurted out, "Domination, yes, I like to watch people being dominated."

Lester smiled and said, "You are my kind of girl. I, too, love the sense of pain mixed with pleasure."

As Lester led Michelle deeper into the area, Michelle's mind scrambled for some plan that would allow her to break free of Lester's pursuits without drawing attention. They approached a doorway, and as they entered, Michelle observed a man tied up in the center of the room naked with his hands stretched out and bound by ropes as his legs appeared to be shackled to the ground. A beautifully shaped woman dressed in black leather with boots extending to her knees had the man's cock in her hand while she spanked his ass with a whip and shouted jesters into his ears. Michelle had read stories concerning domination but found the firsthand interaction appealing.

The woman screamed at the bound man, "Don't you fucking cum, I'm not done with you yet," as she jerked his stiff meat, bit his ear, and spanked his ass hard.

"Yes, lover, I will not cum. Please spank me harder?" pleaded the man.

Michelle found her curiosity had begun to take over, and she felt a rush of blood shooting through her body while stimulating her pussy as Lester pressed his presence close to her body. She tried hard to keep her mind focused but often became lost while watching the woman torture the willing man's body in a painful way but with sexual methods that resulted in pleasure. Michelle became stimulated as she observed the dominating woman strap on a fake dick that appeared long while positioning herself behind the man who begged to be fucked. She aggressively shoved a gag ball into the man's mouth as she pulled his hair back and screamed, "You want my big dick in your ass?"

The man nodded his head in a yes motion as he moaned loudly as she started to slip the cock into his ass while stroking his erection from the back. Michelle felt more blood pumping through her body as she watched the woman fuck the man hard in his ass while precum began to drip from his dick.

Michelle became embarrassed when she caught sight of Lester rubbing the outside of his pants, revealing a hard dick. She visually scanned the room and noticed many people enjoying the view of the man's ass being dominated by the woman. Michelle began to slip slowly to the rear of the room as she noticed Lester had pulled out his dick and was in full motion of beating off while enjoying the show. She exited the room while Lester remained focused on the domination and entered quickly into another room, trying to lose Lester. Michelle stepped in and caught sight of a woman standing between two nice-looking men nude with both her hands extended out with their cocks in her hands.

Michelle sat in one of the unoccupied seats toward the side of the room in the hope of Lester leaving the area so she could explore. Her attention quickly became drawn to the two men and the one woman who started to kiss deeply as they rubbed her body while placing her between their bodies. The woman dropped to her knees and took one cock in her mouth while the other man pulled her ass in position and started to slide his meat into her pussy. Michelle found the sight stimulating and enjoyed watching the man's dick pushing deep in her pussy while she sucked hard on another dick.

Michelle tried to exit the room but found herself drawn to the three fucking as the two men began to reposition the woman onto a man lying on the floor while on his back. The woman knelt while reaching between her legs and grabbing his cock and allowing it to slip into her pussy as she started to ride his body. The other man stood over the man's body and directly in front of the woman, who continued to grind her pussy on the man's cock. The woman grabbed both standing men's ass cheeks with her hands and shoved his dick deep into her mouth as she worked both cocks at the same time. Michelle found herself unconsciously rubbing her breasts and squeezing her legs together as she became intensely stimulated. She almost sighed out loud when she observed the standing man grabbing the woman's grinding hips and slipped his cock into her pussy while joining the same area as the other cock. Michelle was excited to hear the woman's moans as two dicks filled her pussy, opening to its max while two sets of hands grabbed her tits, face, and hips while extending a look of extreme pleasure.

Michelle was focused intensely on the action and found she had given into the sexual energy of the room. She noticed an attractive man sitting adjacent to her with his shirt unbuttoned and exposing his well-chiseled body while he slowly stroked his cock. Michelle found herself becoming tempted to surrender to her sexual desires, and as she watched the woman scream out in pleasure of being double stuffed by two large cocks, she began to lust for the man's dick to be in her mouth. Michelle could almost feel the texture of a hard dick stretching open her mouth while a strong hand pulled her hair while guiding her motions. She imagined the feel of his large balls in her hand as she ran her tongue around the head of his hard cock. Michelle was almost losing control from the onset of a lack of sexual interaction from her relationship with Xavier for nearly eleven months and desperately wanted to feel the presence of a man's cock within her body. She slipped her hand between her legs and found her pussy to be soaked with pussy cum and moaned lightly as she touched her swelling clit and began to masturbate.

Michelle found her legs began to open wide while allowing the presence of her hand to stroke her pussy deeper as she saw the man from behind the woman pull out his wet dick and shoot cum all over her back. She longed for the feeling of warm cum splashing onto her back and imagined she was pinned between the two men taking all their loads deep into her body. Michelle began to feel her body was about to cum as she squeezed her legs together and conjured the courage and strength to run out of the room.

Michelle felt tears building in her eyes as she exited the room and backed her body up against a wall while covering her face. She had become victim to the resurfacing of her past and wanted to feel the presence of a man with extreme urgency. Michelle's mind reminded her of Xavier's intimate phone calls late at night and provided her with the strength to push away from the onset of temptation. *I have to get a grip on myself,* thought Michelle.

Michelle turned and started to head back to the lounge, and to her surprise, she stopped when she overheard a familiar voice saying, "Well, what do we have here? It looks like Michelle has come out to play tonight."

Michelle turned her body as she caught sight of Carl standing directly behind her with a cocky smile on his face.

"I would have never imagined running into your hot ass here, Michelle," stated Carl.

Michelle froze as if she saw a ghost while a rush of confusion and panic cascaded through her body. "I, well, uhmmmmm, came with a friend who was here a second ago, but somehow, we got separated," said Michelle as she tried to cover up her lie and sound somewhat convincing.

"You look fucking amazing," stated Carl as he studied Michelle's body up and down while slightly licking his lips as if he was about to devour her flesh.

Michelle did not know what to do at this moment. *What the fuck, this motherfucker, really? Of all the people, how did I run into this dickhead?* thought Michelle.

Carl moved close to Michelle and said, "Look, I know we were not on good terms the last time we saw each other, but I would like to change that tonight. We have a history whether you want to admit that or not. We fucked, and obviously, we want the same thing tonight or we would not be here, right?"

Michelle pulled herself together and suddenly gained a significant amount of confidence when she caught the sight of Carl's gold badge as she remembered how Lester said it could get you access to the lower levels.

As Carl moved within inches of Michelle's body and took his finger and touched Michelle's chest while dragging it down between her breasts, he said, "Can we let our last conversation go and start over?"

Michelle wanted to grab Carl's creepy finger and snap it in half but considered the possibility of trying to convince Carl to take her to the lower levels after she tries to persuade him. Michelle knew this was her way to access where the senator's wife may be held and could use Carl's obsession with her as her bargaining method.

"Carl, you were a complete prick when I ran into you and your wife at the grocery store," firmly stated Michelle.

"Okay, I'm sorry, you have to understand. You are the most beautiful woman I have ever seen, and I want to be with you again!" said Carl.

"The way you spoke to me was degrading, and what makes you think you can have my ass again acting like that?" said Michelle. "Anyway, you hoped on top of me for less than two minutes on your sofa and blew your load on my tits and ran, looks like you weren't too focused on having some more of me," said Michelle.

Carl placed his hand on Michelle's shoulders and said, "I fucked up. I was afraid my wife, who was also your best friend, would wake up and catch me fucking you."

Michelle knew this was her chance as she had him begging for her and said, "You're going to have to impress me then. What I have seen in these rooms is not enough for me to forget and spread my legs again for I was just about to leave," said Michelle.

Carl desperately pleaded with Michelle to please stay and give him a chance to make things better as he wanted nothing more than to be inside Michelle once again. "Enough then, buy me drink," said Michelle.

Carl led Michelle out of the area and approached a stairway that leads up just above the lounge while flashing his gold badge that allowed access to the site. Carl asked Michelle to sit as he flagged the topless waitress to take their drink order. Carl ordered a Long Island iced tea while Michelle asked for a Bud Light in a bottle. Carl caught sight of Michelle's long legs crossed while sitting and became excited at the sight of her white thigh-high pantyhose while lusting after her cleavage that gave a view from her large breast size.

Michelle knew she had to play this perfectly and strategized on how she could tempt Carl and lead him on without having to engage sexually with him. *How the fuck am I going to do this when Carl thinks he is about to fuck me again?* thought Michelle as she caught view of Carl flashing his gold badge at the waitress who seemly did not charge for the drinks because of his position.

"You wanted to get away and play tonight, Michelle?" asked Carl.

"My friend asked me to come and see what I thought about the club," said Michelle.

"What do you think so far?" asked Carl as he took a big drink out of his glass.

"It's okay. I'm not really into the stuff I have seen so far. I can fuck a woman anytime, see someone get spanked, or find two willing guys to give me their dicks, so it's just okay," stated Michelle.

Carl felt as if he was about to shoot his load as he listened to Michelle say she could fuck multiple guys or even women and said, "Michelle, what would you like to see?" Carl moved closer to Michelle and placed his hand on the outside of her leg and leaned close to her ear, saying, "I can make any of your desires come true, just asked, and I will make it happen."

Michelle knew she had to give a little to get what she wanted. Michelle brushed her hair to the side while revealing her sexy neck and rubbed Carl's legs just inches from his balls and said, "I like to watch people being very rough and fucking nasty. That will make me wetter than anything," explained Michelle.

Carl smiled as he ran his hand up Michelle's leg and tried to kiss her. Michelle turned her head and said, "No, you are going to earn this ass, so show me something crazy hot."

Carl grabbed Michelle firmly around her throat and said, "You fucking tease, I like that. I'm going to shove my big dick so deep down your throat you will be begging for me to cum."

Carl stood up and walked over to a couple of men standing next to a doorway and spoke quietly for a minute. Michelle took several deep breaths and considered her plan if Carl would take her down to the lower levels. Carl walked back over to Michelle and asked her to follow him. Carl led her over to the two men who opened a door, inviting the two to walk through. The doorway led to an elevator that displayed several levels, including a basement and subbasement levels.

The door shut as Carl entered. He turned to Michelle and said, "Now you have to give me something if you want more."

Michelle almost panicked as she thought quickly about what she was going to allow. She was not in the position now to piss him off. Michelle reached forward and placed her hand on the outside of Carl's face while giving him a small kiss on his cheek and said, "Show me something hot, and I will go a little further."

Carl's blood rushed deep into the depths of his dick while wanting to take Michelle right then and there and said, "Push the subbasement, I guarantee you will find something to your pleasing," said Carl as he swiped his gold badge through a reader that allowed access.

CHAPTER 21

Michelle's heart beat faster while anticipating what may be behind the elevator door once they open and what Carl would try to do in exchange for allowing her access to the lower levels.

"I want you to suck my dick, Michelle," said Carl.

"Carl, I need something from you first. Just because we have talked and had a couple of drinks does not mean I have forgotten how you treated me," said Michelle.

Michelle knew her request was not enough and required a drastic invention. Michelle grabbed her dress folds between her large breasts and pulled open her shirt that revealed her massive breast and their pierced nipples while giving into Carl's deepening lust for her flesh.

"Fuck, they are more beautiful than I remember," excitingly said Carl as the elevator dinged and the door opened slowly.

Carl grabbed Michelle's hand as she closed her dress top and pulled her out into a darkened area that was dimly lit while she overheard screaming and what appeared to be the sound of pain. Carl grabbed Michelle by the waist and then cupped both his hands onto her ass cheeks and said, "Now tell me what I have to do to find my way into this nice ass?"

Michelle allowed Carl to bite and suck her neck as he fondled her ass while thinking about what to say as she tried to control the onset of being attracted to Carl. "I'm not sure, show me what's down here."

Michelle could feel Carl's hard dick pushing into her belly area as he was forcefully trying to pursue her. Michelle pushed Carl back and said "Show me" with a firm voice.

"Okay, this way," said Carl as he smiled and let out a creepy laugh.

Michelle followed Carl while looking around and observing stone-textured walls with wooden doorways and walls lined with flaming torches that helped light the pathway. Michelle could hear the screams becoming louder as they ventured deeper into the location. Carl stopped at two large wooden doors and pulled them open, allowing the moans and cries to become much more relevant. Michelle observed a large room with what looked to be a throne sitting within the center with several nude men and women chained around the base.

What the fuck is this shit? Am I going to make it out of this? thought Michelle. Michelle grabbed Carl's hand to make him stop walking and asked, "Carl, what is this place?"

"This place, Michelle, is what you asked for. Now let us stop the bullshit and tell me what you want to see," said Carl.

"Force, aggression, taboo, and brutal!" shouted Michelle. She let out the only thing that came to mind that might be enough to convince Carl that she wanted something extreme.

"You want to see someone getting raped," asked Carl. "You are kinkier than I thought, Michelle. I knew you were a little fucking whore, but now I'm interested," said Carl.

He led Michelle toward a doorway on the left side of the throne area, and as they were about to enter the entrance, the door came open and entering were two men dressed in robes. Carl turned and forced Michelle on her knees, saying, "Get on your fucking knees and bow."

As they both knelt, Michelle moved her eyes and witnessed a man she had never seen enter the room. His demeanor was cold and evil while possessing a frame well above any man she had ever witnessed. He had two long horns protruding from his head while covered in leather clothing as he passed by in front of the two. Michelle hid her face just as he turned and looked at her and Carl. Michelle began to tremble with fear and started to experience difficulty breathing as she realized the man was the bull the senator described that kidnapped his wife.

No, no, no, this can't be happening. Why did I do this? thought Michelle as she started to develop a sense. She was not going to be able to get out of this place alive.

Michelle was relieved as the massive man and his followers passed them and took his throne. Carl stood up and led Michelle out of the large room into another area where she could hear screams as if they were almost in front of her.

Michelle stopped Carl and asked, "What the hell was that?"

In a voice of excitement, Carl turned and said, "You have witnessed the bull. The bull is magnificent and rules this domain."

Michelle looked at Carl as if he had lost his mind and said, "Really?"

Carl turned to Michelle and asked, "Do you want to meet him?"

Michelle appeared to be excited but trembled with fear and said "You fist, Carl" as she winked and motioned him to keep moving.

Carl was pleased to hear Michelle wanted to pursue her pleasures and led her into a dark room only lit by the light of a torch where a dark-haired woman was screaming while a cloth gag with tightly covered leather straps bound her mouth tied to a tabletop naked with her hands. She was positioned with her ass toward her and Carl as they stood in the middle of the area while she tried to escape the clutches of the binds.

Michelle could see the woman was not the senator's wife and told Carl, "I want to watch you forcefully fuck a woman of my choice."

Carl looked deeply into Michelle's eyes and said, "Come with me."

Carl grabbed Michelle by the hand and moved his hand in between the folds of her dress top while sliding around to her back, which exposed her left breast. Michelle could feel the cool of the air, causing her nipples to become erect while her anxiety began to increase as she felt an overwhelming sense of danger.

Carl pushed Michelle forward as he whispered in her ear, "I'm going to take you to a special place that only a few get to experience. It becomes important that you keep your mouth shut and never share any details of what you're about to experience. If you do, we both will be held responsible."

Carl removed his hand from the exposed area of Michelle's body and grabbed her by both shoulders with a firm grip and said, "Michelle, this place is a privilege and an escape where people like us can explore our deepest desires without consequence, but I warn you, down here there is no justice system, and if you share the secrets of this place, you will never see the light of day again. Do you understand?"

Michelle looked at Carl and said, "You're scaring me."

Carl smiled and said, "You should be scared and stimulated as well as fucking horny. I'm about to blow your mind and then fuck your pretty ass off."

Michelle and Carl walked toward a doorway that had steps that led downward in a spiral. As they descended, they came to a door where a man stood guard and discreetly spoke to Carl. The man looked at Michelle with a lustful approach and opened the door for them to enter. Carl entered first while Michelle followed with trembling knees. Once her eyes started to adjust to the darkness of the area, Michelle saw several women gagged and bound by leather straps in various regions. The sound of hard fucking and screaming caused Michelle to turn her head as she observed a naked man viciously fucking a woman from behind while ramming his dick hard in and out of her body as she was laid over a stone feature. The man let out a scream as he appeared to cum inside the woman's body while continuously slapping her ass area.

"Do you like what you see, Michelle?" whispered Carl into her ear as he softly licked her earlobe and rubbed her ass.

"I do. I want to see the women up close so I can choose the one I would like to watch you fuck," said Michelle.

Carl led Michelle to the first woman with light hair who looked as if she had been beating severely while lying almost unconscious and saw it was not the senator's wife. The woman had marks on her back that appeared to be cut from being whipped while her legs were stretched open and cum dripped slowly from her pussy onto the floor, forming a small puddle.

"Not this one," said Michelle.

Carl led her to two other women whom she said she did not find appealing to her liking, and then a side door opened, and Michelle caught the sight of the senator's wife lying on her side as a man walked out of the room.

Michelle could see it was who she was looking for and said, "I like the blond in the room. Can I see her up close?"

Carl led Michelle into the room and asked her, "Is this what you like?"

Michelle's eyes connected with the senator's wife's eyes as she began to realize she knew who Michelle was by how she expanded her eyes and started to moan loudly. Michelle grabbed Carl, spun him around quickly, made his back face the senator's wife, and pressed her lips hard onto Carl's face, allowing him to kiss her deeply. Carl aggressively pulled open Michelle's dress and exposed her bare breast as he firmly took them both in his hands while forcing his wet tongue into Michelle's mouth.

Michelle pushed Carl back and said, "I want to play with her first."

Carl almost looked as if he hit the jackpot as excitement flushed his body. Michelle asked him to undress, sit, and stroke his dick while she played with the woman. As Carl began to pursue naked-ness, Michelle turned her body to face the senator's wife and held her finger to her mouth, indicating that the senator's wife needed to remain quiet. Michelle pulled her dress over her shoulders and allowed her nakedness to be revealed as the dress fell to the floor. She felt an overwhelming feeling of vulnerability as she started to bend forward and straddle her body over the senator's wife.

Michelle turned her head while placing both her hands close to each side of the senator's wife's head and leaned forward while whispering in her ear, "Please go with this. I'm here to help and get you out of here."

The senator's wife rubbed her head against Michelle's face to indicate she understood. Michelle leaned up, and Carl moaned as he started to stroke his dick as he caught the sight of Michelle's large breasts brilliantly hanging from her chest while her ass curved outward, revealing her perfect curves. Michelle rubbed her hands over the senator's wife's face and squeezed her breast as she moved her hips forward and backward, pretending she was riding a dick. Michelle knew she had to be convincing, or Carl will start to suspect something was up.

"Kiss her, Michelle," demanded Carl.

Michelle removed the gag from the senator's wife's mouth and began to kiss her mouth lightly. Carl was pleased with the show he observed and furiously beat his meat harder as Michelle turned to Carl and said, "Don't you fucking cum, I want you to fuck her very hard and shoot your tasty load onto her breast so I can lick it up."

Carl responded with, "Fuck yeah, both of you bitches are about to get this big dick. Michelle, I have waited a long time to fuck you again."

Michelle kept her eyes locked onto Carl and his dick as she slid her tongue up and down the senator's wife's body as she began to finger herself for Carl's enjoyment. Michelle took a deep breath and conjured the courage to place her mouth onto the senator's wife's breasts and begin to suck them with a sense of aggression.

Carl stopped masturbating and said, "You are so hot, Michelle. I was about to shoot my load everywhere. My turn."

Michelle became overly tense and was not ready for Carl to pursue the senator's wife; she quickly started establishing a plan.

Carl walked over to Michelle and the woman, placed his hand firmly onto Michelle's ass, rubbed down the back of her leg while putting his erect dick into the woman's mouth, and demanded her to start sucking. The senator's wife closed her eyes tightly and started to suck his dick with intensity from the side while trying to make him feel good while Michelle slipped off her body. Carl reached for Michelle as she pushed his hand onto the senator's wife's body.

"Now, show her you're the fucking man, and she's just a piece of worthless ass for fucking," commanded Michelle.

Michelle slid up behind Carl's naked body as the senator's wife sunk her mouth deep onto his dick and grabbed his hips, guiding his dick and moving him in and out of her mouth while telling Carl, "Fuck her whore mouth."

Carl was overwhelmed with excitement and moaned loudly as Michelle rubbed his body from behind and the woman sucked his hard dick.

"Carl, I want you to fuck her and punish her for being a whore," whispered Michelle.

Carl leaned his head back and said, "Yes, mistress, I will do as you say."

Michelle knew she had him where she wanted and slipped back as Carl released the straps from the senator's wife and stretched open her legs. "Untie her hands and let her fight you as you fuck her hard," said Michelle.

Carl stopped for a moment while holding the senator's wife's legs open and stared at Michelle. *Oh no, is he catching on?* thought Michelle.

"You never know what lies in the darkest parts of a person's mind. You will enjoy this, Michelle," stated Carl.

Michelle was relieved to hear Carl agreeing to her demands as he unloosed the ties from the senator's wife's hands. Michelle shook her head at the senator's wife and gave her a look of urgency as Carl's head was turned, untying the other hand. The senator's wife looked terrified as she appeared to trust Michelle's plan. Carl leaned back as he squeezed her breasts and made the senator's wife jack him off. The senator's wife let out a scream as Carl slapped her backhanded and shoved his dick hard into her body.

Carl fucked her violently between her legs while forcing his hard dick deep into her body. The sound of skin smacking was loud as the woman screamed from the onset of the intense pain sliding in and out of her body. Michelle stood silently and observed how fast and hard Carl fucked the senator's wife as she caught sight of how he was focusing on the woman's breast. Carl stopped abruptly and flipped her over, making her get on her knees as he aggressively gripped her hips and fucked her from behind. Carl let out a loud moan while his head leaned back as he prepared to cum inside her body. Michelle waited patiently for this moment as she picked up the wooden chair, and with all her might, she swung the chair, striking Carl hard in the back of his head and causing him to fall onto the senator's wife's body.

The woman cried out loudly as she pushed Carl off her body as he fell to the hard flooring with a stream of blood protruding from the rear of his head. Michelle stood in shock as she held the broken piece of the shattered chair. The senator's wife pulled herself up slowly due to her weakened state and cried as she reached for Michelle.

Michelle dropped the remaining piece of chair and held her tightly, saying, "I'm sorry he had to do that, I had to wait for just the right moment, or he would have overpowered me."

The woman held tightly to Michelle as she cried and said, "You came. No one else has tried to help me. Thank you."

CHAPTER 22

Michelle pulled the senator's wife's body up into a standing position and leaned her up against the table while grabbing her dress, slipping it back on, taking Carl's shirt, and placing it onto the senator's wife's body. Michelle attached the gold-level access badge to her dress, grabbed one of the long leather cords, and stuffed it into her purse.

"You have to listen to me and follow my every move if we are going to make it out of here alive," stated Michelle.

The senator's wife's face streamed with tears as she quickly nodded her head in agreement. Michelle placed the senator's wife's arm around her shoulder and helped her to the doorway, where she opened with much caution. She peeked around the corner and knew she could not exit the way she entered due to the number of people she encountered while nervously remembering her encounter with the bull. Michelle muscled the senator's wife to her side and proceeded down the darkened hall to the left. The two of them moved quickly to the corner as they heard people talking and coming through a distant door.

Michelle and the senator's wife help each other as a party of four men passed by while talking loudly and using profane language describing the acts they had just committed. One man said, "Did you see her fucking face when I slide my dick into her ass? You would think I had a fourteen-inch dick." The men continued to brag about their encounter.

Michelle stood steady, and as the men passed, she continued to the doorway the men exited through. She swiped the badge and heard the door beeped and opened. She pulled the door open slowly and peeked through the small opening, which revealed another large room that contained a woman laying over a structure on her belly with her hands tied to the floor in a motionless position. Michelle placed her hand over the senator's wife's mouth as she witnessed blood flowing from the woman's ass and down her legs, which caused her to react with panic. Michelle scanned the room and did not detect another door but noticed a curtain protruding down the wall behind the woman. She noticed the curtain moved slightly and moved to see what was behind the covering. Michelle covered the senator's wife's face to shield her from the sight of the woman whose eyes were open and seemed to be dead.

Michelle kept thinking about Xavier and seeing his face as she imagined while she kept pushing the woman through this endless maze of horror and sex. She pulled the curtain slightly and observed a door with a small amount of light shining from underneath. Michelle sat the senator's wife down on the floor and proceeded to get down on her knees and look under the doorway. She did not detect movement and repositioned the woman back into her clutch and swiped the door badge, which opened the door. Michelle and the woman entered quickly as they overhead a noise behind them and quietly shut the door. She turned and found a stairway going up and started to climb the many steps while helping the senator's wife up the challenging grade. The stairway took them to another set of doors, and Michelle decided to open the door to the right. As she swiped the badge and unlocked the door, she stepped in and saw several sets of people engaged in sexual acts around a large pool with an environment that contained much humidity and steam.

The room provided Michelle and the senator's wife an opportunity to rest for a bit as Michelle laid her down and positioned herself on top of the woman, looking as if they were engaging in a sexual act.

"Rest for a moment, and we will try to find a way out of this room," whispered Michelle into the woman's ear.

Michelle looked to her left and observed a woman riding a man lying on his back while another woman straddled her pussy over his face and noticed a doorway toward the back of the room. Michelle noticed the area directly behind the three people fucking was dark and provided the best possible path to move toward the door on the other side of the room. Michelle cautiously moved the senator's wife into the darkened path and slowly made her way past several people involved in sexual acts. The doorway was just feet from Michelle and the woman. Michelle pulled the woman quickly toward the door and swiped the badge and promptly exited the room. She found herself back in the first hallway, where she and Lester entered the room and observed the woman fucking the man whom she was dominating while tied up.

She had to make a quick decision and decided to head down the hall to a doorway set off from the other. She pulled the card down the access slide, and it turned red, causing her to feel a great deal of panic. Michelle could hear a woman's voice just on the other side of the door, pulled the senator's wife to the side with her back toward the door. As the door opened, Michelle grabbed the door and pulled herself and the woman inside while the waitress passed quickly through holding several drinks on a tray. Once inside the room, Michelle and the woman froze as they came face-to-face with two topless waitresses preparing drinks in a kitchen-style setup.

"Can we help you with something?" asked one of the women.

"My girlfriend is sick and about to puke. We're trying to get outside quickly before she throws up everywhere, too many drinks and sex," said Michelle.

Both waitresses looked at each other and possessed an expression as if they did not want to deal with the woman getting sick in their space and told Michelle to go through a door they swiped. Michelle saw an alley with dumpsters and boxes while pulling the senator's wife out and moving her with great haste as the waitress closed the door.

"Were out, were out," whispered Michelle to the senator's wife as she hurried to pull the woman toward the end of the alley.

Michelle felt a rush of adrenaline as she knew she survived and rescued the senator's wife from certain death if she had not been recovered. Michelle was just feet from turning the corner when she felt someone pull her hair from behind.

"You fucking bitch, you hit me with a fucking chair. You are going to wish you never met me," said Carl as he found Michelle and the senator's wife.

Carl pulled Michelle's hair with great force to the ground as he raised his fist and struck the senator's wife in the jaw, causing her to fall to the ground. Carl pulled Michelle to her feet and forced her up against the wall as he pulled her hair backward and licked her neck. Michelle tried to fight but could not overpower the strength of Carl as he kicked her legs open and placed his leg between her thighs, causing her to stay open.

Carl yelled into Michelle's ear and said, "You're going to meet the bull after I fuck your pretty ass, Michelle. This did not have to come to this. All I wanted was to play." Carl continued to say, "You know what's happening. You're going to die now bitch, you fucking whore."

Michelle stopped resisting and said, "Okay, please I will do what you want."

Carl stopped his pursuit and turned her around and said, "Yes, you will. Now you're going to suck my dick right here and now."

Carl pushed Michelle aggressively onto her knees, unbuttoned his pants, and pulled out his dick that extended just inches from Michelle's mouth. Michelle resisted as Carl grabbed her hand and tried to place it on his dick. Carl pulled her hand hard while slapping her firmly with his other hand, causing Michelle to stream long trails of tears as she proceeded to grip Carl's hard cock into her hand and opening her mouth.

"Yea, cry all you want, bitch, the next thing that will flow is my thick load down your throat!" said Carl as he screamed at Michelle.

No, thought Michelle as she pulled his dick upward with great force and struck Carl's balls from underneath with great power, sending Carl collapsing in pain to the ground. Michelle stumbled as she tried to get away from Carl as he grabbed her feet and restrained her from moving.

"Oh, you bitch, that's it. I'm going to fuck your asshole so hard you will wish you were dead!" screamed Carl as he pulled himself up.

Michelle screamed as Carl threw her body face first into the brick wall while tearing her dress off her body and pushing his body forcefully onto hers that did not allow her to move.

Michelle pushed hard backward as he finished ripping her dress from her body. Carl reached around Michelle and shoved two of his fingers into her pussy and finger fucked her pussy hole deeply, causing a great deal of pain to shoot through Michelle's body as he squeezed her throat area tightly with his hand.

"Scream, you little whore, no one is going to save you," said Carl as he removed his fingers and showed Michelle her wetness as he placed the two fingers in his mouth and swallowed her juices.

Michelle felt an overwhelming sense of anger, lunged her head back, and busted Carl's nose, sending blood dripping down his chest as he screamed with pain. "Fuck you, you bastard, just fucking kill me then!" screamed Michelle as Carl stood up in front of Michelle and punched her twice in the face, causing her eyes to roll back as she passed out from the sudden blows striking her face.

Carl threw Michelle's naked body over a trash can and positioned himself behind her body as blood dripped onto her back and screamed, "Now you're getting it, bitch!"

Michelle's body lay motionless as Carl grabbed his dick while stroking it fast and started to place the head of his dick into Michelle's ass and started to push it in when he suddenly felt his body being dragged backward.

Carl turned his body as he moved backward and struck the person pulling him in the right eye. The two men began to wrestle while falling to the ground, where Xavier jumped onto Carl and began to punch him with a forceful blow to his face. Xavier pinned one of Carl's arms under his leg and continued to hammer down devastating fist blows to Carl's face as he began to blackout. Xavier jumped off Carl as he felt his adrenaline pumping and moved fast to check Michelle's pulse to discover she was unconscious.

Xavier started to pick up Michelle's bruised, bleeding, and naked body as he caught sight of another man running down the alley. Xavier placed Michelle on the ground and positioned himself into a fighting position as the man loudly said he was with Michelle.

"Stop, please, my name is Jordan, and I'm with Michelle here to rescue the senator's wife. Is Michelle, okay?" said Jordan as he pleaded for Xavier to withhold his advancement.

"She's hurt but breathing. What's going on here?" asked Xavier.

Jordan checked on Michelle and quickly moved to pull the senator's wife to her feet and to drag her out from the alley. "You need to leave this place now. They will kill you if they catch you. No police. Here's my card, call me. Michelle will also explain!" shouted Jordan.

Xavier pulled off his shirt, grabbed her purse, and covered Michelle's nude and broken body as he moved quickly toward his truck parked around the corner. Xavier pulled open the door to his vehicle while laying Michelle's unconscious body into the passenger side. Xavier started his truck and pressed the gas firmly, casing a screaming sound roaring from his back tires. He was confused and did not understand what was happening or why Michelle was in the facility with another person in a back alley, nude and being sexually assaulted. Xavier felt angry and relieve that he found Michelle and pondered why he could not contact the local authorities. Xavier decided to take Michelle back to his place to care for her and figure out what was happening.

CHAPTER 23

Michelle opened and closed her eyes slightly as she began to regain her consciousness. She was confused and tried to determine her whereabouts as her eyes were cloudy, feeling a significant amount of pain shooting through her body.

"Michelle, Michelle, can you hear me?" rang a familiar voice into Michelle's ears.

Michelle tried to sit up but quickly collapsed due to the onset of her traumatic event that took a tremendous toll on her body. "Xavier, is that you?" Michelle started to cry out from the onset of pain and trauma.

"It's okay, I have you. You're safe," said Xavier in a calm, low voice as he rubbed Michelle's face with a cool towel and held an ice pack to her face.

Michelle began to regain her eyesight and discovered she was lying in Xavier's bed while tightly covered in warm blankets. She tilted her head to the side and saw Xavier looking at her and tending to her injuries.

"Here, take a drink," said Xavier as he placed a straw into Michelle's mouth while she began to drink slowly.

Michelle coughed slightly and asked, "Where is the senator's wife?"

Xavier took a deep breath and stated, "I'm confused as to what was happening. A man named Jordan who I saw you leave your house with took the woman and told me she was the senator's wife. I think we need to talk once you feel up to explaining."

Michelle reached out her hand and placed it onto the side of Xavier's face and said, "How, where did you come from, and you said you saw me leave with Jordan?"

Xavier held Michelle's hand tightly and explained he was on his way to pick her up for their date when she called and said something came up and needed to cancel. "I had a nice bouquet in my truck, and I was just a few minutes out and was going to leave them at your step. When I arrived and stepped out my truck, I saw you dressed beautifully while getting in the car with the man Jordan," explained Xavier. He continued to explain how he became upset and confused about what he witnessed and decided to follow them to their destination.

"I care deeply for you, and the sight of you leaving with another man upset me. I had to know if you were seeing someone else," explained Xavier.

"It's not what it seemed. I can explain, I'm sorry," said Michelle as she started to cry once again.

Xavier took a cloth and cleaned the tears from Michelle's face and said, "When you arrived at that place and stepped out of the car with the man, I became furious and thought you were on some date," explained Xavier. "So I became angry and drove off and sat at a store for several hours, and when I calmed down, I decided to drive back by the location and saw the car was still sitting in the parking lot," said Xavier. "That's when I heard you scream. I was unsure as to where you were exactly, but I ran around the entire building, and when I turned the corner, that's when I saw you being assaulted," explained Xavier.

"You saved me. Are you hurt?" asked Michelle as she noticed Xavier had a black and swollen eye.

"No, just a little mark from our altercation," said Xavier.

"The last thing I remember was Carl attacking me and trying to rape me while I slammed my head back into his nose," said Michelle.

"It appears he struck you several times in the face, causing you to pass out, and when I caught sight of you when I turned the corner into the back alley, he was trying to penetrate you from behind, so I jumped on him and fought till I was able to get you free," said Xavier.

"I have some explaining to do," said Michelle in a desperate tone.

"When you're ready, Michelle. Let's focus on getting you well. We can talk about this when you feel better," said Xavier.

"No, I must explain this now," said Michelle as she pushed her body upward and laid her back against the headboard of his bedding.

"If you're wondering, I had to give you my shirt, and, yes, I gave you a sponge bath and tended to your wounds. I'm sorry if that offends you. I tried not to look," said Xavier as he winked at Michelle.

She giggled and grabbed her jaw from the onset of pain. "How bad is my face?" asked Michelle.

"Swollen, bruised, and cut, but you're still beautiful," said Xavier as he parted her hair over her ear and gripped her shoulder.

Michelle pulled Xavier close to her body and gave him a tight hug and said, "You are amazing, and thank you for coming back for me."

Xavier gave Michelle a soft and lengthy kiss and said, "I love you, and something deep inside me encouraged me to go back there. If I would not have listened to my intuition, I don't know what would have happened to you."

Michelle told Xavier how she knew Carl and said they had a one-time affair and was deeply ashamed of her actions. "First, I'm not dating Jordan. He is the friend of a senator and his wife," said Michelle.

"Wow, you have no idea how relieving it is to hear you say that," said Xavier.

Michelle continued to explain how she had provided therapy services for the senator and his wife for the last several years and had gotten to know the couple very well while developing a close bond with his wife.

"The stories I shared with you on the night we met were the senator and his wife," said Michelle. "So you can see how twisted their lifestyle has become and how they have consulted within me to help them sort out their newfound path," explained Michelle.

She began explaining how the senator called her and pleaded with her to help him due to his position within the community and how it would damage his career if their information became known to the public. "A significant amount of me wanted to contact the police, but the senator pleaded to please help him retrieve his wife so this could be kept out of the view of others," said Michelle.

She continued with detailed information concerning her interactions and actions while in the discreet location, providing all the details to help Xavier understand her intentions.

Michelle lowered her face forward and said, "Xavier, I would never do anything that would jeopardize our relationship, but I had to do a few things I'm ashamed of to rescue the senator's wife."

Xavier placed his head against Michelle's and said, "Look at me, you are the bravest person I have ever met. I was angry when I saw you with another person when we were just minutes from our date, but I'm relieved to have you here at this moment, so you do not have to tell what you would do in a time of crisis."

Michelle looked at Xavier and said, "We have been together for almost eleven months. These eleven months have changed me and showed me a different way to love someone. Transparency has to be included in our relationship if we want to move forward."

Xavier smiled at Michelle as he continued to tend to her injuries and care, saying, "We can talk about things we will do later. It's good to have you here."

Michelle became amazed every time she was within the presence of Xavier, and for once in her life, she felt accepted, safe, and empowered.

"I hear what you're saying, Xavier, but the fact is, you do not know everything about me and the things I have done," said Michelle.

"On the contrary, you do not know everything about me either, Michelle," stated Xavier.

"You make a great point. I place myself within a spot in my life to where I feel ashamed of the things I have done," stated Michelle.

"The things we have done and experienced are what makes us who we are, don't you agree?" asked Xavier.

Michelle thought about Xavier's statement for a minute and said, "You're right. I give the same advice every day, but for some reason, I tend to think of myself as different when in fact I'm just like everyone else."

Xavier lifted Michelle's cup to her mouth and encouraged her to drink more liquids and said, "You have been through a lot. We have much to discuss, but the time is now. We could just drop everything and run to a whole new life if we wanted. What has happened is in the past."

Michelle continued to feel an overwhelming need to confess her past to Xavier and said, "No, I need this, so here it is. I love sex and everything that goes along with it. I have slept with many men over the years. I have built my life around my work and never wanted to settle down and used men and women to provide a way for pleasure."

Xavier rose and looked at Michelle with a serious glare while Michelle became nervous about how Xavier would respond to her confession. "We all have sexual desires and done things we are not proud of. You don't think I have not made some of the same mistakes? I spoke with my father concerning several things within my life. He gave me great advice to follow."

Michelle looked at Xavier and said, "What did he say?"

Xavier smiled and said, "My father told me how he met my mother and how certain things become difficult, but forming a relationship without sexual contact would reveal a true mate." Xavier continued to explain, "He said the best things in life are earned and worth waiting for and require much time to establish."

Michelle thought about Xavier's words as he continued to care for her needs and said, "If the son is like the father, then I have found my pot of gold."

Xavier was pleased to hear Michelle's statement and gave a soft kiss on her lips and said, "I am sorry, but I will have to leave today and follow up on my story concerning the missing persons. Please call if you need anything."

Michelle thanked Xavier as he left and bundled up tightly in his covers and tried to rest while reflecting on the past event.

Xavier's contact sent an urgent message saying he had some inside information on a recent body found in an alley behind a local building. Xavier traveled to the location where his contact shared detailed knowledge of how a woman was found naked and displayed several signs of sexual battery. Xavier's contact had access to a photo taken by the police that showed how the body was discovered and provided detailed images of the scene. Xavier listened as his contact explained how the body was positioned in a prostate potion within a spray-painted image of what appeared to be a silhouette of a man with horns on the brick wall.

Xavier studied the photo and compared it with the actual painting before him on the wall, and as he noted the details within his voice recorder, he paused suddenly. He thought, *Wait, could this be connected to Michelle's situation?* Xavier noticed the woman's back had some marks while quickly pulling out his magnifying glass to discover that the markings appeared to be bite marks.

Xavier looked at his informative and slipped him some cash and said, "Thank you, I have to go. Can I keep the photo?"

The informant agreed Xavier could keep the photo, and Xavier rushed to head back to his home to compare notes.

CHAPTER 24

Michelle was lying in Xavier's bed and became startled as she heard a loud bang. "Xavier, is that you?" shouted Michelle as she waited silently for a response and listened for the sound of his voice. After a couple of minutes, Michelle began to become paranoid and decided to make her way out of bed and see if she could discover where the sound originated.

As Michelle stood on the hardwood floor, she noticed her head was a bit wheezy and held onto the side of the bed for a moment while seeing something out of the corner of her eye passing through the sight of the living room.

"Xavier, is that you? Please who is here?" pleaded Michelle as she began to develop a deep feeling of fear.

Michelle walked toward the darkened living room. As she approached the doorway of Xavier's bedroom, she stopped suddenly as she caught sight of a darkened image in the background that rose and revealed a silhouette of the man from the discreet club who appeared as the bull. She began to tremble and could not move her body from the onset of panic while she felt urine running down her legs from the sight of the presence whose eyes glowed red and began to move toward her.

Michelle covered her mouth with her hand as she began to move back toward Xavier's bathroom as the presence moved slowly toward her, revealing its image within the light of the room.

"No, no, stay the fuck away from me!" shouted Michelle as the light showed the man with the horns from the discreet club they called the bull.

"Did you think you could come into my domain and take away my property?" said the bull with a deep voice.

"I have a gun. Stay the fuck away from me, or I will use it!" shouted Michelle as she became terrified as to what his intentions were.

"You can't kill me, you can't run from me, and you can't hide from me. I know and will be able to find you anywhere you go," said the bull as he stood just feet from Michelle.

She grabbed Xavier's lamp and hurled the object at the beast. As he rose, his hand swatted it from his path while reaching forward and grabbing Michelle by the neck and lifting her off the ground. Michelle could feel his enormous strength tightly around her neck as she kicked, punched, and held the horns of the beast, trying to free herself from his tight grip.

Michelle felt her breathing becoming restricted as the beast held her high in the air. She noticed his teeth were pointed while his body displayed enormous muscle form as his eyes looked evil and colored in red. Michelle struggled to wiggle free but realized his power was too much as he threw her onto the wall, causing her to crash to the floor as pictures and drywall broke around her body.

Michelle felt her hair being pulled with much effort and let out a scream as the beast shouted, "I take what I want, and now, I'm going to take you as mine!"

The beast dragged Michelle by her hair across the floor with his right hand while grabbing her foot and throwing her onto Xavier's bed. Michelle tried to exit off the other side of the bedding as she felt the beast grab her legs and pull her back toward him with her belly on the bedding. She felt the beast's fingers entering her shirt collar as he tore open her shirt from the back, revealing her naked body. Michelle screamed for help and tried to pull her way off the bedding but could not break the hold of the beast.

Michelle cried loudly as she felt the beast sliding his tongue over her ass and toward her shoulders while pushing her body down into the bedding, causing her to become helpless. She screamed at the top of her voice as she felt the intense pain of the beast's teeth sinking into the flesh of her back. Michelle felt as if his enormous weight was going to snap her body in half as she started to feel him pulling open her legs from the back and placing his hand onto her head while her face sank into the mattress.

"Fuck, stop!" screamed Michelle as she felt the opening of her pussy spreading as the feel of his large penis began to sink into her body.

Pains electrified her body as the presence of his dick bottomed out inside of her body and began to forcefully slide in and out of her pussy. Michelle's body jerked and moved with significant actions as the beast pounded his hard dick in and out of her body while holding Michelle tightly to the bedding as she pleaded for him to stop. The beast pulled Michelle's head back with her hair and flipped her tiny body onto her back as he mounted her on top and reassumed his dick, invading her broken body.

Her legs felt as if his force was going to rip them from her body as he brutally rammed mercilessly deep into the depths of her body. She felt pain spreading through her right breast as he sank his sharp teeth into her flesh while blood began to flow down toward her belly. All Michelle could do was cry and pray the intrusion was about to stop while experiencing the onset of extreme penetration with the most significant-sized dick penetrating her pussy.

The bull pulled Michelle's legs over his shoulders as she gasped from the size of his dick sinking into her pussy deeper while his balls began to smack hard onto her bare ass cheeks. Michelle's pussy popped and spewed cum that leaked onto the bedding while her opening stretched to its limits. She turned her head to shield herself from his demonic facial expressions as he smiled and ran his tongue over her chest. Michelle concentrated her pains onto a picture of Xavier on the wall as her body moved violently from the beast's intrusion. The bedding sounded as if it was about to break as the headboard pounded hard against the wall.

The beast pinned Michelle's hands above her head as he fucked harder than ever as saliva dripped out of his mouth and splashed onto Michelle's face. He moaned and started to change his action as he pulled his large dick from Michelle's body and leaned back and jerked his fluids onto her body. Michelle shielded her face from the onset of his massive cum bursting as his hot load splashed onto her belly, breast, and covering her neck area. Michelle caught sight of the beast pulling his length back and forth as he dumped every drop onto Michelle's body. The beast lowered his position as he finished his cum and slipped his dick back into Michelle's pussy that sent pains flashing through her body once again while he pulled a knife from his side and pushed it deep into Michelle's chest, causing her to scream and cry out for help. The cold blade pierced her chest, causing blood to pour out of her body and onto the bedding. The beast leaned back while laughing and started to pull off his facial skin that looked like stretchy plastic while revealing Carl laughing loudly and saying, "I got you bitch."

Michelle jumped from her bedding while holding her chest to the sound of her phone ringing on Xavier's end table. Michelle felt as if she could feel the blade and presence of the beast as her heart beat quickly and her body shook in terror. She covered her face and discovered the encounter as a dream while feeling a tremendous amount of relief.

Michelle grabbed her phone and answered, "Hello."

She heard a familiar female voice that said with urgency, "Michelle, this is Lucy, Carl's wife."

Michelle became nervous as to how this conversation was going to proceed and listened carefully.

"I am calling everyone I know. Carl has not been home in two days or has called me. It is usual for Carl to stay out for a night now and then, but tonight will be three nights since I saw him," said Lucy with a panicking voice. "If you happen to run across him, please tell him to call me," stated Lucy.

Michelle took a deep breath and tried to control the sound of her voice and said, "Lucy, I will and hope everything turns out okay."

Lucy sat for a minute and said, "I'm afraid he might be seeing other people."

Michelle was torn, and withholding information was complex for she knew that Carl was a cheater and said, "I'm sure he's just thinking things over concerning the new baby, and surely, he will call you soon."

"Michelle, I miss you and hope you are doing well. You were a good friend to me, and I dislike how life consumes us and causes us not to be able to spend time together," stated Lucy.

"Lucy, I will call you if I run into Carl. You might need to contact the police and make a missing person's report," said Michelle.

"I have already called the police, and they said I would have to wait for three days and then call back," stated Lucy.

Michelle could see that Lucy needed to talk to someone, but today and under the circumstances was not the right time. "Lucy, I wish you well and hope you find Carl. I have to go. Please call me if you need me," said Michelle as she hung up the phone. Michelle sent word to her company and receptionist that she had an emergency and will not be returning to work until after one week.

CHAPTER 25

One day earlier, Carl opened his eyes to being surrounded by several men, hung nude and suspended from the ceiling. A rope tied Carl's hands, and his body hangs inches from being able to touch the ground within a darkened room. Carl moans loudly as he feels the pressure of a man striking his stomach area with their fist. The club manager walked up to Carl, kneed him hard in his penis that sent Carl into excruciating pain while he grabbed his face with a firm grip.

Carl cried out, "What the fuck are you doing?"

The man looked at Carl and began shouting in his face, "You don't fucking talk! I ask the fucking questions!"

Carl closed his mouth and nodded his head in agreement while the man started to speak. "It appears one of our girls found you unconscious in the back alley with your dick hanging out, so she asked the staff to pull you back in, so we couldn't make sense of what happened." The man turned Carl's head back and forth and observed Carl's cuts and bruises while asking, "Who did this to you?"

Carl blurted out, "I don't know, I was leaving, and someone jumped me from behind. That's all I remember."

The manager waved his finger in Carl's face and began to make snaping sounds with his mouth and said, "It just so happens I pulled the video footage of the back alley and observed some interesting actions, Carl."

The manager walked around Carl's suspended body as Carl began to plead, "I'm sorry, she got out and took a woman with her. I tried to stop her, you have to believe me." Carl began to tremble with fear as he knew the manager had caught him in a lie.

The manager struck Carl's face violently and screamed, "You fucked up, Carl, over a piece of ass. I saw you trying to fuck the woman outside the club while causing a significant amount of attention to be drawn to our place."

Carl screamed once again as the man struck him four times in the belly and once in his side area. Carl tried hard to regain his breath and said, "Please I can tell you who she is, but I don't know who the guy was that jumped me from behind."

The man looked at Carl and said, "Oh, you will fucking tell me, and the woman that she took out of here was a senator's wife. You messed up badly, Carl."

Carl cried out, "I'm sorry, I messed up. Her name is Michelle and close friend of my wife."

The men began to laugh as Carl continued to plead for his life while they caught the sight of Carl urinating onto the floor as his body trembled out of control. "I'm glad you said that, Carl, and listen to me fucking carefully. If you do not bring me Michelle and the senator's wife back, I am going to take your wife to the bull and watch him fuck her harder than you have ever seen."

Carl pleaded, "I'll do it. I will get them both back. Please do not hurt my wife?"

The manager struck Carl's body once again and said, "One chance, Carl, one chance, and if you do not bring her to me, I will fucking kill you and make your wife a fucking whore."

The manager looked at Carl and laughed out loud as he walked out, saying, "Do not touch this Michelle. Bring her to me. I want to taste her myself before sending her down."

Carl felt the rope being cut above his head as his body fell to the hard flooring. Carl wept out loudly as anger began rushing through his body as he held his side from the onset of pain that took over his body. Carl grabbed his clothing that was thrown in his face as the men exited the room.

Carl found his way to his feet as he slipped his clothing back on and headed back to his home. As Carl exited his vehicle in his driveway, his wife ran out crying and embraced him with a tight hug, saying, "What happened? Why are you beat up? I have been worried sick."

Carl gripped Lucy's shoulders and asked her to please get back in the house as he looked over his shoulder with paranoia and locked his door while closing all the curtains.

"Carl, you are scaring me. What is going on?" asked Lucy.

Carl grabbed a handgun from a drawer and said, "I'm in trouble, cannot explain now. I need you to shut the fuck up and pack a bag and go to your mom's house until I reach back out for you."

Lucy looked terrified and said, "What have you done?"

Lucy shielded her face as Carl lifted his hand as if he was going to backhand her face, saying, "Can't you do as your told? I don't have time to explain, and I have something I must straighten out, or it's going to get worse. Now pack and go."

Lucy quickly departed to her bedroom crying and began to pack as Carl limped into his bathroom and found his way into a hot shower that washed the blood from his body.

Once Carl cleaned and nursed his wounds, he found a fresh set of clothing. While exiting the bathroom, he saw Lucy had packed and left for her mother's house.

Fuck them and fuck Michelle. Oh, I'll bring her back, but I'm going to fuck the shit out of her first and to hell with who attacked me. He's got one coming, thought Carl.

He grabbed a bag and packed duct tape, strap ties, and rope while finding the contact book that revealed Michelle's phone number, home address, and business location. Carl ripped the page from the book and shoved it into his pocket as he slammed his home door and headed toward his vehicle. The vehicle rear tires let out a screeching sound as Carl spun the tires and headed toward Michelle's workplace. Carl sped into the parking lot of Michelle's workplace and stopped his car in an accessible parking spot just outside the door as he put on a hat and dark sunglasses while grabbing his bag.

Carl exited the elevator onto Michelle's office floor and approached her receptionist who said, "Hi, can I help you?"

Carl stopped in front of her desk and could see Michelle's office door was open and lights were out and firmly said, "I need to see Michelle now."

Michelle's receptionist looked at Carl and said, "She will not be in until late next week. Can I help you with something?"

Carl turned quickly and headed back to the elevator, shouting, "You're no fucking help!"

Carl slammed his car door and headed toward Michelle's apartment while becoming overfilled with anger and thoughts of abusing Michelle's body. Carl parked his carl onto the curbing while grabbing his bag and running into the foyer toward the elevators. He rushed into the first opening elevator door while almost knocking down a woman who said, "Watch out, man."

Carl stuck his middle finger up to her as the elevator doors began to close and said, "Cunt."

Once he approached Michelle's door, he knocked loudly with extreme force. He knocked for several minutes and then looked right and then left to see if the halls were clear and kicked open Michelle's apartment door.

Carl entered Michelle's apartment quickly and began searching every room and realized she was not home. He grabbed his phone and called Michelle's cell phone. Carl slammed the phone when she would not answer and began to throw Michelle's items throughout the apartment. He made his way to her room and emptied every drawer item onto her flooring as he found her panties in which he smelled and licked the crotch with his tongue while ripping every piece of clothing out of her closets. Carl found one of Michelle's sexy dresses and laid it out on the bedding while unzipping his pants and pulling out his dick. He wrapped a pair of Michelle's lacy panties around his shaft and stood over her dress and began to jack off with intensity. Carl remembered how good Michelle felt as he fucked her on his sofa while he started to shoot his load all over her dress. He milked every drop onto her dress as he stuffed the lacy panties into his pocket and zipped up his pants. Carl went back into the living room, sat discreetly at Michelle's window area, and waited to see if she would return.

Several hours have passed, and Carl was beginning to become more frustrated about where she was and if she would be returning home. Carl searched Michelle's home for any indication of where she might be but could not find anything that would provide a clue to where she might be staying. Carl dumped Michelle's bedroom nightstand onto the flooring and found her diary.

Well, what do we have here? thought Carl as he scanned through the pages and observed intimate details of Michelle's life. He turned toward the rear portions of the journal and found Michelle talking about Xavier and how he lived out in the country on a farm.

"Here we go. Got you now, bitch!"

Carl saw an insert that provided an address to Xavier's home. Carl jumped up, stuffed Michelle's journal in his jacket pocket, and took out his knife while carving offensive slurs into Michelle's walls as he exited her apartment. Carl's anger continually hardened his heart, and revenge was all he could think of now.

Michelle has fucked up my life and status at the club, and when I get her back, I'm going to fuck her every day. She will get hers, but first I need to make a little stop at the senator's house, thought Carl.

CHAPTER 26

Xavier began to travel back home while pondering many thoughts concerning a connection between the sex club and the missing women. *Michelle described in detail how she was told about a bullish figure and bite marks displayed on women's back. The picture I have possessed the same type of injuries and has a spray painting of a bull on the wall,* thought Xavier. He pulled his vehicle to the side of the road and spoke into his voice recorder for several minutes while recapping things Michelle told him and details concerning the murder scene.

"I am finding there might be a connection between the club and the murders," said Xavier as he closed his voice recorder. Xavier found the business card Jordan handed him while in the quick exchange within the alley and decided to give him a call.

"Hello, this is Jordan," said the voice on the other side of the phone.

"Jordan, my name is Xavier. I'm Michelle's boyfriend. Do you have a minute to talk?" asked Xavier.

"Yes, absolutely, anything for a friend of Michelle. I remember you from the alley and have heard many good things about you," said Jordan.

"First, how is Michelle?" asked Jordan.

"She is doing much better but has several bruises and cuts and has been through a lot," explained Xavier. "How is the senator's wife?" asked Xavier.

"Thank you for asking. She is not doing too well. Due to the down low of the current situation, she is having a difficult time dealing with the traumatic experience. As you may know, she was raped continually and beaten badly," explained Jordan. "Xavier, I am aware you are part of the media, and the senator can only ask if you could respect their privacy and let him handle the situation due to his standing within the community," asked Jordan. "The senator would be willing to supply you and Michelle with an ample amount of compensation for your secrecy," said Jordan.

"I understand and will try to abide by your asking, but I need to ask you a question," said Xavier.

"Please, anything," said Jordan.

"I think the murders within the community may be connected with the club. I need to know if the senator's wife had any bite marks on her body?" asked Xavier.

"Many on her back areas that looked as if a sharp-toothed animal bit her," explained Jordan.

Xavier explained how he observed other victims had similar marks while describing the bull silhouette spray-painted on the alley wall.

"Our interactions within the club have revealed a being known for aggressively fucking women and leaving deep bite marks on their body, but to our knowledge, we thought the activity was a show and stagged until the senator's wife was abducted," explained Jordan. "I will let you know that the senator made a mistake and tried to strong-arm the club personnel and got ruffed up badly while they revealed camera footage of him and his wife's interactions within the club to be used as blackmail," said Jordan.

Xavier placed his hand on his forehead and said, "I think this whole situation may be deeper and more dangerous than we originally thought, and I think Michelle may be in greater danger than I thought," said Xavier.

"Please let us know if we can help you and hope Michelle is safe and okay," said Jordan as he ended the call.

Xavier knew the club more than likely had Michelle's identity and footage of her interactions within their club. Xavier called

Michelle and explained the phone conversation he had prior with Jordan and made her aware he was confident the club and the murders are connected.

"Please keep the door locked tight and do not answer your phone for anyone until we figure this out," said Xavier to Michelle.

"Xavier, I'm scared," said Michelle.

"Michelle, I love you very much, and I will not let anyone harm you," said Xavier. "Michelle, I will call you back in a few. I have another call coming in from Jordan and need to take the call," said Xavier.

"Hello, this is Xavier."

A moment of silence and sniffling became the exchange between Jordan and Xavier as he felt his intuition alarming him that something was wrong.

"Jordan, what is wrong?" asked Xavier.

"They're both dead. I found them both strung up naked and hanged by their stairway just over the entrance foyer," cried Jordan.

"Who, who is dead, Jordan?" asked Xavier.

"Both the senator and his wife," said Jordan.

Xavier sat for a moment and said, "I'm sorry, have you contacted the police?" asked Xavier.

"Yes, they are on their way. Can you please come here and help me sort this out?" said Jordan.

"I'm on my way," said Xavier.

Xavier arrived at the senator's mansion to find a slew of law enforcement coming at the scene. Xavier caught sight of Jordan and made his way to him and waited for several minutes as officers were taking statements and beginning to investigate the scene.

As Jordan finished his brief remarks, he walked out toward the center yard fountain with Xavier and hugged him while slipping a small envelope within his pocket and whispered in his ear, "I made you a copy of the surveillance footage. We need to bring these bastards down. Don't trust anyone, they have connections on the inside," said Jordan.

Xavier nodded his head as he listened to Jordan, providing him firsthand knowledge of what he discovered. Jordan explained he was supposed to meet with the senator and his wife concerning the recent events, and when he arrived and walked into the home, he was met with a horrific finding. Jordan explained how the senator and his wife were hanged to death by a rope attached to the top of the stairs and hanging directly over the foyer space. The bodies were naked and appeared to be savagely beaten while blood pools collected under the bodies on the granite flooring.

"I know this was them because there was a symbol drawn in the blood of a bull on the chest areas of them both," explained Jordan.

"What are you telling the police?" asked Xavier.

"Nothing but me finding them hanging from the ceiling when I was entering the home. I am not going to mention the tie-in with the club. If we do, we will surely be next," said Jordan.

Xavier could do nothing but think about Michelle and her being alone and began working hard writing down information and trying to extract information from the police.

Xavier's informant was on the scene, pulled Xavier to the side, and shared several details concerning the investigation.

"Xavier, the detectives have discovered a pattern concerning the markings left at the murder scenes and how they are starting to suspect all the bodies are victims from a serial killer," said Xavier's informant.

"Do they have any leads or decisions to the whereabouts of the killer?" asked Xavier.

"All we know is the bodies are similar and contain the mark of the bull image," said the informant.

Xavier slipped the informant a note that contained the address to the club. "What is this?" asked the informant.

"Check this out. I think your victims will all connect to this location. You must be careful to who you share this information," firmly explained Xavier.

The informant looked at Xavier and said, "I will head over that way and see what I can come up with and will let you know if I discover anything," said the informant as he walked away.

CHAPTER 27

The informant who worked for the police department decided to withhold sharing the information and headed toward Xavier's location he provided. The informant pulled up to the building next to the dock area and circled the building while discovering no visible markings to indicate what the building represented.

"Dispatch, this is 427. Can you verify if a business exists at 1036 Triad Way?"

The radio beeped after about two minutes. "Negative on the location containing a registered business, but records show a Cornelius Fantom is the owner of the property," said dispatch.

"10-4," said the informant as he observed the building and noticed several cameras located around the higher portions of the building. The informant exited his police cruiser and began to walk around the building, checking if he could pick up on any unusual activity when he noticed a man leaving from a doorway several feet from where he was standing.

He decided to approach the doorway while noticing all the windows were tightly covered and allowed no visible access into the interior portions of the building. As he approached the entrance, the door opened, and the manager asked if he could help him with something.

The informant pulled his police badge and showed the man his credentials while asking, "Do you mind if I ask you a few questions and is it okay if we sat and speak within your office?"

The manager looked hesitant as the informant picked up quickly on the man's hesitation to let him enter the complex. "Can I ask what this is about?" asked the manager.

"Yes, sir, I am investigating the recent murders in the area and trying to collect as much information as I can," said the informant.

"Not sure what that has to do with me, but give me a minute, and we will sit and talk," said the manager as he smiled and entered back into the building.

The informant glanced around his surroundings and began to think, *Something is not right here. What is in this building?* He reached for his walkie-talkie and started to contact dispatch for backup. As he rose his walkie-talkie to his mouth, he began to press the call button. The manager opened the door and asked the informant to please enter.

"Thank you, sir," said the informant as he placed his walkie-talkie back into the clip on his belt without informing dispatch for additional backup.

The manager led the informant down the darkened hall while entering through a doorway that took them to his office. "Please have a seat. My name is Cornelius. How can I help you?" asked the manager.

"May I ask what this building is used for and does it contain a business?" asked the informant.

"What does my building have to do with your investigation of a crime, Detective?" asked the manager in a rude fashion.

"Like I said prior, we are investigating all leads about the recent murders and going door to door trying to collect information," said the informant.

The detective noticed the manager was hesitant to provide any information and wondered why there were so many cameras if there was no business within this location. "I notice you have several cameras located throughout and were sitting in an office, what do you do for a living, Cornelius?" asked the informant as he leaned forward to listen to his reply.

Cornelius was cunning and thought carefully about how he was going to reply to the detective's question. "I'm sorry, I don't mean to be rude. The truth is, I'm starting a storage facility and have not applied for the proper permits due to lack of funds."

The detective nodded his head in agreement and said, "Well, I would have to say, the interior of this building is nice for someone who does not have the funds to apply for business permits."

Cornelius stood up and opened a cabinet on his back wall and grabbed a cigar while trimming the end and striking a match to light the end, saying, "Detective, I'm an honest man trying to make a living, come with me, and I will show you around and prove to you I run a legitimate operation."

The detective stood up and started to follow the manager.

The manager led the detective down the long hallway while his cigar smoke clouded the area and said, "Look, what's your price?" Cornelius stopped and turned around and said, "Everyone has a price. What is your price to turn around and leave me alone?"

The detective responded, "You understand it's a crime to bribe a police official, right?"

Cornelius laughed and began to open a doorway, saying, "Sorry, officer, I was joking, please come in, and I will show you what we do here."

The detective walked in while looking upward due to the shortage of light, and when he looked into the remaining parts of the room, he noticed a woman who was naked and bound to a table on her back with her legs spread wide open.

"What the fuck is this?" asked the detective as he quickly reached for his weapon. The detective froze the pursuit of his gun as he felt a hard pressure against the back of his head and the sounds of a revolver clicking a round into a chamber.

"Okay, we do not need to do this. I'm a detective, you prick."

Cornelius walked around the front of the detective and asked, "Does your department know you are at this address?"

The detective became nervous and said, "I did call in and verified if the location was a business."

The manager shoved the detective on his knees as another man behind him held a weapon to his head and removed his walkie-talkie and handgun. "Now, call in a different address for verification, or I will blow a hole through your body and dump you to the sharks!" screamed Cornelius.

The detective took the walkie-talkie and said, "Dispatch, this is 427. Can you verify the following address at 9210 East College St.?"

The walkie-talkie beeped and said, "427, the location is verified ownership under Ben Wilcox and contains a business license for the manufacturing of car parts, over."

Cornelius pulled the walkie-talkie from the detective's hand and said, "Exceptionally good. You almost cracked the case. Now you will see what we do here."

The detective observed Cornelius speaking to another man who suddenly left the room. The detective noticed the woman on the table was gagged and looked at him in terror. *What the fuck have I done? No one knows I'm here*, thought the detective.

Cornelius giggled like a schoolboy when the door began to open across the room, saying, "Great work, detective, now you are going to meet the bull up close and personal."

The detective tried to pull himself loose from the grip of men as he observed the massive man walking into the room.

"What the hell are you?" asked the detective.

"Shut your fucking mouth and bow your head to the bull," said Cornelius as he struck the detective in the jaw with his fist. "Show him what we do here," said Cornelius as the bull untied the woman and threw her to her knees in front of the detective.

The bull grabbed her hair and pulled her hair back while rubbing his massive penis up and down her pussy opening. The detective became terrified as he observed tears flowing from her eyes while this mammoth-sized man with bullhorns began to violate her body sexually.

Cornelius got behind the detective and whispered in his ear, "Do you like what you're seeing? This is what we do here. We entertain our guest."

The woman screamed through her mouth gag as the bull pushed his penis into her pussy and began to fuck her hard in front of the detective. The detective noticed how the bull licked his lips and violently fucked the woman's body while the men held his head and made him watch.

"Now, touch her tits," ordered Cornelius.

"Fuck you," said the detective as he struggled to break free. The detective stopped his pursuit of gaining freedom as he felt the cold presence of metal pressing into his neck area.

"No, no, touch her tits, or I will cut you wide open," said Cornelius.

The detective let out a cry of fear and placed his shaking hands on the woman's breast as he felt them moving back and forth from the intense pressure of the man fucking her from behind.

"See, that feels good. Enjoy her body and watch this magnificent beast fuck her hard," stated Cornelius.

The detective could hardly watch as they firmly held his head into position. "I bet that feels better than your wife, detective. Do you want to sample her pussy?" asked Cornelius.

"Never, you will not get away with this!" shouted the detective.

"On the contrary, I have already got away with it. See, your captain visits my establishment regularly. We are well-covered," explained Cornelius. "Let's say he loves to fuck women without their consent while they scream and plead for him to stop," said Cornelius.

The detective continued to hold the woman's breast as the beast viciously fucked her body from behind. The beast let out a roar as he sprayed his ejaculate deep into the woman's pussy while throwing her to the ground as he finished. The woman tried to run as two other men grabbed her and laid her back on the table while restraining her hands. The detective felt the men pull him to his feet and began to strip his clothing from his body while positioning him directly in front of the woman's spread legs.

Cornelius gripped the detective's head and pushed him close to the woman's pussy that was leaking the bull's cum and said, "Now, eat her pussy."

The detective resisted and struck Cornelius with an elbow blow, causing him to fall to the ground. The other men began to attack the detective while punching and kicking his naked body.

"Stop, he's mine!" shouted Cornelius as he pulled off his shirt and unzipped his pants. "Hold him down and force his face into her pussy," commanded Cornelius.

The detective fought hard but lost the battle of trying to escape as he felt the woman's pussy pushing onto his mouth and experiencing the taste of the bull's cum in his mouth.

"Eat her pussy!" shouted Cornelius as the detective hesitantly opened his mouth and inserted his tongue into her cum-filled pussy.

The detective let out an intense cry as he felt Cornelius aggressively penetrating his ass with his hard dick.

Cornelius fucked the detective extremely hard with deep penetrating strokes that caused him to plead for Cornelius to stop. The detective's body jerked uncontrollably as Cornelius violently fucked his ass and pressed his face into the woman's wet pussy. Cornelius reached around the detective's body and squeezed his balls while stimulating his penis to an erect state.

"No, please," desperately asked the detective as his body was being invaded.

Cornelius let out a deep moan as he released his seed into the detective's body while laying over his back. The detective felt Cornelius pull his long cock from his ass as warm cum leaked down the inside portions of his legs, collapsing to his knees in pain.

The bull walked over to the detective, lifted him from the ground around his neck, and held him to the wall as he gasped for breath.

Cornelius zipped his pants and said, "What we do here is a service to mankind. I'm sorry you will not live to see the light of day or understand our purpose."

The detective screamed as the bull sank his sharp horns into his chest cavity while penetrating his heart. Blood trickled out of the detective's mouth as he took his last breath while his body fell to the floor.

CHAPTER 28

Hot steam began to roll out of Xavier's bathroom as Michelle decided to clean herself. Michelle undressed and stood in front of Xavier's mirror and examined her body closely. She noticed her black eye and several facial cuts due to Carl striking her face and how her knees were scrapped due to throwing her about the alley. Her neck also showed signs of bruising due to Carl placing extreme pressure trying to hold her down. Michelle began to feel much better, but she noticed her skin was sensitive to touch as she examined her face. She stepped into the shower and slowly allowed the hot water to trickle down her body while noticing the cuts began to sting. Michelle placed her hands against the wall and tilted her head back as water splashed her face and beaded down her curved back. She began to scrub her body with intensity, trying to remove any remains left by Carl. The water felt so refreshing and not only therapeutic, but her standing naked in Xavier's space sent waves of pleasure and left her with a sense of security.

As Michelle finished cleaning her body, she wrapped her brunette hair in a white towel and slipped on Xavier's shower robe. While standing in front of Xavier's sink, she caught sight of something passing by the bathroom window at a quick pace. She tried to make out the image, but she could not determine if it was a person or just an animal due to the steam. *Stop, Michelle, you are so paranoid, just focus on cleaning up. No one could know where you are*, thought Michelle as she allowed the robe to drop to her feet and removed the towel while beginning to blow-dry her hair. The presence of the warm air flowing through her hair reminded her of her ATV ride with Xavier and how she wanted nothing more than to finish their roll in the hay. As Michelle finished drying her hair, she grabbed one of Xavier's disposable razors, rubbed shaving cream around her vagina, and began to manicure her heart-shaped pubic hair. Even though she was physically damaged, Michelle could not fight her ongoing sense to have Xavier ravish her body and take her away from all this trouble.

Michelle finished up her bathroom duties and decided to ask Xavier if he would stop by her apartment and grab some of her clothing, makeup, and personal items. She picked up her phone and text the information to Xavier, saying, "Hey, sexy, could you stop by my apartment and pick up some of my items? I will text my landlord you are stopping by, and he will provide you access. Call me when you arrive, and I will walk you through what I need, chow."

Xavier saw Michelle's text and said, "Michelle, I will be happy to grab whatever you need, but I must tell you something first. The senator and his wife have been found dead at their home."

Michelle covered her mouth as the onset of comfort left her body and quickly replaced it with fear and sadness. "What happened?" asked Michelle.

"Their bodies were found hanging above their foyer by Jordan as he entered the home today, Michelle. I'm very sorry," texted Xavier.

Michelle's body began to shake out of control as tears of sadness streamed down her face. "I just got here out of that horrific place, and now this," replied Michelle. "Please be careful, I do not want to know any more details at this moment. Please come home to me when you can," asked Michelle.

"I'm trying to finish up with the interviewing, and then I will be all yours for the rest of the weekend. I'm truly sorry, Michelle," replied Xavier.

Michelle sat on the toilet and placed her hands over her face and began to wonder if this nightmare was ever going to end. *Everyone around me is dying*, thought Michelle as she tried to make sense of how her life has changed so much in just the past few days. She stood up and walked into Xavier's bedroom where she stood for several seconds while leaning against the wall and caught sight of Xavier's sofa. *Too much fucking stress*, thought Michelle as she began to feel the need to release the significant amount of stress pressure from her body. She remembered how Xavier stroked his long cock on the sofa with a quick pace and recalled the image of his cum spurting into the air and running down the back of his hand and onto his balls. Michelle began to feel an overwhelming need to cum while she allowed her robe to fall to the floor and positioned herself onto the sofa in the same place where Xavier pleasured his cock.

Michelle spread her legs wide open as she caressed her left breast and started to rub her slightly wet pussy. She began to arch her back as the waves of pleasure began to flow through her body as she stroked her pussy fold. Michelle loved sex and missed the presence of a lover desperately. As she rubbed her pussy faster, she imagined Xavier suddenly catching her naked on his sofa and unzipping his pants and stroking his dick while standing beside her. Michelle could feel the soreness of her injuries, but the mixture of pain with pleasure provided a comforting escape from all the mess she has encountered lately. She consistently rubbed her moist spot over and over as her sighs began to turn into moans of pleasure as she pushed her hips up and down while finding the right location that sent her the most pleasant sensations. Her mouth was completely open, and she consistently licked her lips as she imagined the feeling of Xavier's hot cum splashing down onto her chest. She curled her toes as she arched her head back and began to release a sound of pleasure as her juices began to flow out of her pussy and covered her fingers. Michelle screamed as her orgasm pulsed through her body and hardened her nipples.

Michelle slowed her movement as her body began to jerk from the onset of sensitivity while imagining she was looking into Xavier's eyes as she rubbed her fingers through his load and sucked the cum from her fingers as he finished covering her body with his load. Her pussy was swollen and had spurted liquid out onto the side of her leg that sent chills throughout her body. Michelle licked her wet pussy cum from her fingers as she squeezed her legs together and twisted her ass onto Xavier's sofa. She would be willing to give Xavier anything he desired at this moment if he was to catch her masturbating on his sofa and demanded her body.

Michelle turned and placed her hands on the back of the couch and positioned her knees on his cushions while placing her ass out into a fucking position. She could feel the weight of her large breast pulling her chest down and the feeling of cool air brushing across her exposed ass as she laid her head against the back of the sofa and dreamed of Xavier sliding his long dick into her body and using her pussy to cum. She slowly twitched her ass back and forth as if she was teasing a big cock and soaked in the moment of her body rushing with warm blood while experiencing an overwhelming feeling of sexual energy.

She jumped to her feet and covered her body as she thought she heard something coming from outside. Michelle moved toward the front door and peeked out the small window and did not see anything or anyone moving about the area. She walked over to the side window next to the pool area while slipping her robe back on and thought she saw something move along the side of Xavier's parents' home. Xavier's parents were out of town and not due back for several days. She quickly darted to his room and grabbed her phone and began to text Xavier. "Hey, is someone supposed to be at your parent's house doing any work? I thought I saw something moving about the outside of the house." Michelle dropped her robe and slipped on Xavier's sweatpants and pulled one of his shirts over her body while placing a hat onto her head as she placed her feet into his flip-flops. She quickly ran back into the living room and peeked discretely out the window curtain for several minutes while not seeing any more activity.

Michelle glanced at her cell phone several times, hoping that Xavier would see her text message but did not see a notification where he read her text. She began to build a little strength to open the side door and walk out onto the pool area in the hope of trying to get a better view of what was happening over at his parents' home. Michelle stood for several minutes and did not see any more movement and decided to move a bit closer and peek into the garage side door. The sun was beginning to set as Michelle moved within just a few steps of the door; she jumped from the floodlight kicking on and held her hand to her chest to help control her heart rate. The garage looked undisturbed as she moved past the kitchen window and viewed into the dimly lit house. Michelle looked down as she stepped onto a metal rod and decided to pick it up for some protection. She lifted the rod to her side as if she was about to swing a bat and proceeded slowly around the corner and stepping onto the porch.

The front door looked secure and remained locked as she investigated the window and did not see anything moving around. Michelle began to think she was seeing things and thought, *Okay, maybe my eyes were playing tricks on me due to it getting darker outside.*

She continued to walk around the home and did not see any indication of forced entry or signs of someone on the property. Michelle decided to text Xavier once again, saying, "Sorry, I'm just paranoid. I think everything is okay."

Xavier just saw her text and said, "Are you sure? Sorry, I'm a little tied up with the senator's situation, but I will head to your home as soon as I can. Please call me if you need me."

"I'm good, just heading back and going to try and cook up something to eat. I'll have you something hot and tasty waiting," said Michelle.

"If I'm correct, I would say you were describing yourself," said Xavier.

Michelle smiled as she read his reply while heading back into his house and said, "Okay, naughty boy, I'm not on the dinner menu, but I can be found on the dessert list."

Xavier blushed as he read her text and replied, "I might just have to sample that dessert sometime. I love you."

She shut the door and texted, "I love you more."

CHAPTER 29

Michelle took a deep breath and laid the metal rod next to the front door and decided to take a swim in Xavier's pool before she started cooking. She turned on the pool area lights, slipped off all her clothing, and stepped into the pool fully nude. Michelle did not have a bathing suit, so naked was her only option. She slipped down into the cool of the water while feeling the water rush over her body. Michelle lightly swam across the pool while dipping under several times and touching the bottom. She turned onto her back, relaxed her body while floating, and caught a glimpse of the night sky illuminated with thousands of stars. Michelle thought of how beautiful the stars were and how lucky Xavier was to look into the sky and see them without the lights of a city blocking their spectacular view. Michelle pulled her body to an upright position as all the pool lights suddenly turned off.

"Hello, is somebody there?" asked Michelle with a nervous voice. She let her body drift out into the deeper section of the water while she treaded the water but did not hear a response or any other sounds. Michelle began to feel slightly uneasy with the situation and decided to pull herself from the water and check the light switch outside the house.

As she approached the light switch, she grabbed a towel from the cabinet next to the poolside and wrapped it around her body. *What the hell?* thought Michelle as she noticed the light switch had been clicked in the off position. She pulled the button back up and saw the lights flashed back on and then turned it off once again and realized the switch was working. At that moment, Michelle jumped as she heard thunder in the distance and noticed clouds were beginning to cover the star-lit sky.

I'm going to lose my mind if this kind of freaky shit does not stop. First the figure and then the lights, what's next? thought Michelle as she began to consider that the onset of the storm may have caused the lights to shut off. She moved quickly, picked up Xavier's clothing she had been wearing, and decided to return to his home while closing the door and securing all the locks. Michelle froze utterly in her tracks when she heard, "Well, looks like the cat just found the mouse."

Michelle began to feel her eyes filling with tears and streaming down her face as she recognized the familiar voice while turning slowly to catch a glimpse of Carl standing just four feet from her body and holding a handgun.

Carl's nose had a white bandage taped across it horizontally and displayed black eyes signs due to Michelle's headbutting him a few days prior. "Looks like we have a situation here that needs to be ratified, so I would advise you to sit the fuck down in the chair and shut your mouth!" screamed Carl.

Michelle moved quickly and sat in Xavier's chair while her body began to shake uncontrollably at the thought of what was about to happen. She knew she was in great danger of Carl finishing his sexual assault and possibly taking her back to the private club. She watched as Carl walked around and sat on Xavier's sofa and listened carefully as he began to speak.

"You fucked up, Michelle. All I wanted was your ass, and now you have messed up my position within the brood, and now I have to return you."

Michelle leaned forward and pleaded with Carl to not hurt her anymore. "Carl, I know you and your wife. We all have a history. Please I will fuck you if you just leave me alone," said Michelle as she began to surrender in fear of her life.

Carl looked at Michelle and ran his eyes over her half-naked body. "Yes! I'm going to fuck you, but after that, I have to take you back to the bull," said Carl as he licked his lips and stared at Michelle's body.

"Carl, please, how can you do this to Lucy?" asked Michelle with a shuddering voice.

"Lucy? Yes, she is a nice piece of ass, but the brood within the club gives more than I can ever desire. I can have anything at any time with anyone," said Carl. "Now, I have been snooping about and have found that no one is here to save you, so let's begin. Scream if you want, I like that too," said Carl as he unzipped his pants and pulled out his dick and began to stroke it slowly.

"Remove your towel and throw it to the floor and spread your legs over the side of the chair," commanded Carl.

Michelle took a deep breath and knew this was it; there were no other options. She removed the towel and released it to the floor. Michelle began to feel a rush of anger and fear while she spread her legs and allowed them to drape over the chair arms for Carl to see.

"Damn, even though I want to fuck you up for breaking my nose, I cannot deny you are the most beautiful woman I have ever seen or had the privilege to fuck," said Carl in a creepy voice.

"Fuck you, Carl, you will not get away with this. Xavier will be here at any moment!" screamed Michelle.

"Xavier, so that is who you speak about in your book, and I look forward to finishing my meeting with him based on the last time we met in the alley. This time, it will not go too well for him," said Carl as he began to stroke his hard meat faster.

Michelle knew Carl had found her diary and would do anything to have her willingly fuck his cock. "Carl, okay, what can I do to make this better? Do you want me to suck your dick? I will. Do you want to fuck me? Then let's do it now," said Michelle.

"Michelle, all of the above and more," said Carl.

"Okay, what's first?" asked Michelle.

Carl looked at Michelle's big breasts with lustful eyes and said, "Play with your pussy."

Michelle leaned her head back and began to rub her already moist state as Carl stood up and positioned himself just over her body while beating his length at a fast rate. Carl's pants fell to the floor as he grabbed Michelle's head and made her look at his dick as he aggressively stroked toward his ejaculation. Carl commented on how nice Michelle's breasts were and told her he would bite her nipple rings and stretch them with his teeth when he fucked her. Carl's balls were low hanging and swung in motion as he got off on watching Michelle's hand rubbing over her heart-shaped pubic hair while her fingers became shiny with her pussy cum. Michelle thought hard on constricting a plan and decided to reach out and grab Carl's big balls with her hand as she rubbed her fold.

Carl stopped, pointed his gun at Michelle, and gripped her hand while saying, "Bitch, if you fucking hit my balls again, I will fucking kill you where you sit."

Michelle gave Carl a seductive look and said, "Carl, I have fucked my pussy with my dildo many times, thinking about you ejaculating all over my breasts again. Will you do that?"

Carl responded to Michelle's command with urgency and said "Fuck yeah" as he leaned forward and prepared to cum on Michelle.

Michelle rubbed his ball with precise pressure and watched Carl's eyes as he began to squeeze them shut while starting to moan. Michelle watched as Carl's cock began to shoot out white cum that splashed onto her face and trickled down onto her breast. Michelle's body began to shake, and her adrenaline spiked well beyond anything she had ever felt as she waited patiently for Carl to finish his load onto her body. Carl screamed as the second wave of cum blasted out in complete form and covered her space between her breast while running down to her belly. Carl was in full motion and stroking fast as the third wave hit her mouth area and splattered onto her neck. He aggressively grabbed Michelle by the head and forced his dripping cock into her mouth and gagged Michelle as he penetrated her throat and released some more sperm into her mouth.

Michelle squeezed her eyes tightly shut and placed her hand on Carl's arm as he finished his load into her mouth. Michelle opened her eyes suddenly as she held onto his arm that controlled the weapon and bit down onto Carl's dick with tremendous force, causing him to collapse to the ground as Michelle stood and forward kicked Carl directly in his face, causing him to drop the weapon as he fell screaming to the ground as blood flowed from his penis.

Michelle jumped forward and over the sofa as her naked body slid across the wood floor while grabbing the metal rod and immediately throwing it into Carl's face as he was trying to stand back up. The metal rod struck Carl directly over his nose and right eye, sending him to the floor unconscious. She stood up and screamed as Carl's cum ran out of her mouth, and she began to vomit up his seed that was forced down her throat. Michelle made her way to Carl's motionless body and picked up his weapon as she began to turn for the door and exited. She felt a sharp blow to the back of her head as Carl had grabbed the metal rod and hit her head while sending her body to the floor. Michelle screamed as her eyes became unfocused while her finger fired off the weapons rounds in various potions. Carl jumped to the side, trying to avoid the gunfire as one of the bullets struck him in the leg, sending him into terrible pain. Michelle's body collapsed entirely onto the floor as she passed out.

CHAPTER 30

M ichelle felt her body being pulled as she started to regain consciousness. She felt her hands being bound and pain rushing
down through her body as her arms suddenly were extended upward
and her body hung suspended from the ground. Michelle's eyesight
started to become focused as she observed she was hanging from her
hands in Xavier's barn directly over the hay. She began to shake and
tried hard to free her hands while Carl sat on the four-wheeler and
held his hand over his cock, cursing Michelle.

"You fucking bitch, you almost bit my dick off. What the fuck!"
screamed Carl as he began to walk around the barn. "You are dead!"
screamed Carl as he lifted his harm with his handgun and pointed it
directly at Michelle's face.

Michelle called for Carl to end it as Carl pulled the trigger,
causing the firing pin to strike the round chamber, resulting in an
empty weapon.

"Fuck!" screamed Carl as he realized the gun was out of bullets.

Carl grabbed a metal barrel and filled it with straw and loose
boards as he pulled out a lighter and started a fire. For several minutes, Carl added more and more wood, causing the fire to become
hot while taking the metal rod and placing the end into the fire.
Carl held his cock area as he turned the rod and lifted it occasion-
ally to check for heat it was collecting. When Carl saw the rod end
was cherry red, he pulled the rod from the fire and held it close to

Michelle's face, saying, "Look at you now, all naked and covered with my cum. Now you're going to be marked for the bull where you will live out the rest of your life fucking and sucking thousands of hard dicks."

Carl turned Michelle's body and placed the red-hot poker to her flesh, sending Michelle into a screaming fit as Carl burned her flesh and carved in the symbol of the bull just over her left shoulder blade. Tears flowed heavily down Michelle's face as her skin ached with burning pain as she felt her body hitting the straw floor.

Michelle tried to push her body backward as she screamed in terror as Carl approached her once more. Carl jumped on top of Michelle and began to lick her nipples and pull her nipple rings with his teeth to the point of almost tearing them from her body. Carl forced open Michelle's legs and violently finger fucked her pussy, sending waves of terrible pain deep into Michelle's body.

"I might not be able to fuck you with my dick, but I can fuck your pussy with my hands!" screamed Carl into Michelle's face.

Michelle's helpless body lay limp as Carl's fingers sunk deeper into her body, causing her to bleed while casing his entire fist to forcefully fuck Michelle's vagina. Michelle screamed so hard she began to feel her body locking up to the point she would collapse. As Michelle's body jerked back and forth from Carl's fist deeply embedded deep in her pussy, her hands were positioned just over her head as she felt an object just under her grip.

Carl squeezed Michelle's right breast, sending deep pains as his fist showed no sense of mercy while deeply sliding in and out of her helpless body. Michelle dug her grip down into the straw and pulled the object with every ounce of energy, striking Carl's left eye and penetrating deep into his skull as his body immediately went limp and fell onto Michelle. Carl's blood trickled out of his head onto Michelle's chest as she felt Carl's body took its last breath. Michelle pushed Carl from her body and noticed the object was a long construction nail that Xavier must have dropped while driving them into the barn wood to hang heavy objects.

Michelle let out a scream of desperation as she rose from the ground with her hands still tied and made her way to the barn door as she noticed the sight of car lights approaching the property. The car immediately stopped when the headlights shined onto Michelle's broken, bound, and naked body as she collapsed in the mud as rain fell to the ground.

The car door opened, and Michelle overheard Xavier's voice, "Oh my god, Michelle."

Xavier quickly removed his shirt, wrapped Michelle's body, placed her in the car while freeing her hands, and sped toward the hospital. Michelle tried to explain to Xavier that Carl attacked her and was dead in the barn, but she was going in and out of consciousness due to her weakened state.

Michelle could feel Xavier's hand on the side of her face as he drove the car, saying, "Please, Michelle, stay with me. I'm so sorry, I should have never left you at my house."

Xavier could see blood quickly running from Michelle's private areas and observed her body completely covered in blood. "Michelle, hold on, we'll be at the hospital in just a few minutes," said Xavier.

Michelle's head swayed from side to side as Xavier tried to hold her up while controlling the car. Xavier reached back into the back seat, found a spare shirt, and placed it between Michelle's legs, applying pressure to her vaginal injury. The car screeched to a stop directly in front of the emergency room. At the same time, Xavier laid his hand heavily on the horn that alerted nursing staff to run out to the car and immediately start removing Michelle's body into the emergency room. One of the nursing staff members ordered Xavier to move the vehicle once Michelle was out and asked him to come to the triage desk.

Hospital staff rushed Michelle back into the ER and started preparations to evaluate her injuries while caring for her broken body. Xavier met with hospital staff while revealing the circumstances and story behind Michelle's injuries. Xavier was worried for Michelle and wanted nothing more than to hold her again and take her away from all this pain. He consistently walked the hospital waiting area while waiting patiently for all updates concerning Michelle's status. The local law enforcement arrived after the hospital alerted them of the situation and approached Xavier for questioning.

"Xavier, I'm sorry we have to meet under these circumstances. Usually, you are questioning us, but we hope Michelle is recovering well. Can you please provide some information as to what has happened today?" asked Detective Swank.

"Yes, Detective Swank. First, there is a body at my farm location where Michelle and a man got into a violent exchange," explained Xavier as the detective immediately alerted staff to investigate the scene. "I'm going to have to start from the beginning for all this to make sense," said Xavier.

Xavier began by explaining how the senator and his wife were involved with the sex organization and how Michelle became affected due to her involvement with senator and his wife. The detective was amazed at how Michelle recovered the senator's wife and warned Xavier how dangerous the situation was while placing many people in harm's way. Xavier explained how he saved Michelle from Carl at the club location and placed her back at his home due to her being in danger.

"Detective, you have to investigate the club location before more people are hurt," urgently explained Xavier.

The detective's phone rang, and Xavier observed how the detective listened attentively as his staff reported the scene at Xavier's home. "Xavier, I will need to advise you to please stay in town. Even though I have your preemptive story, everyone is a suspect until we sort this out," explained the detective.

"Detective, thank you for your help. I understand," said Xavier.

The detective walked away and met with the hospital staff where he pulled out a small book and wrote many things down from the conversation.

Once the staff was done talking with the detective, Xavier noticed the detective was escorted back toward Michelle's area. The doctor approached Xavier and explained how Michelle was hurt badly but stable.

"Xavier, she is doing fine and in good hands but has a lot of healing to do for a while," explained the doctor. "The detective needs to ask her a few questions, and then you will be able to visit her," said the doctor.

Xavier was about to lose his mind as every minute felt like an hour passed by for him to see Michelle. After several minutes, Detective Swank approached Xavier and explained how his story collaborated with Michelle. Still, he ordered hospital staff to place her under protective custody and assigned police protection for the moment.

"Xavier, I appreciate your cooperation, and sadly to say, your friend from our department was found dead just moments ago outside the building you have described in your statement. We are fully investigating the situation and need you to remain put within the hospital until further notice. I will need you to please withhold your media communication so it does not interfere with our ongoing investigation," said Detective Swank.

Xavier was devastated and mourned for the detective's family and their friendship over the years. Xavier felt a light touch on his shoulder and looked up to a nurse inviting him to follow her back to Michelle. Xavier quickly jumped to his feet, followed the nurse, and entered the room where Michelle was located. Xavier felt extreme emotions as he viewed Michelle lying on the bed with many cuts and bruises while recovering from the injuries. Xavier was relieved to see Michelle's pretty brown eyes opening and looking at him as she raised her hand toward him.

"Michelle, I'm so glad you're okay," said Xavier as he fell to one knee and placed her shaking hand on his.

Michelle opened her mouth and quietly began to speak to Xavier. "I'm sorry to have put you through this. I'm sorry this all has happened," said Michelle as she began to weep and cover her face trying to hide her injuries.

Xavier placed his hand on Michelle's head and rubbed the side of her face, saying, "I love you beyond measure. You are going to be okay, this nightmare is over, and when you recover, I'm going to take you away from this place and bore you with my nerdiness," said Xavier.

Michelle held her chest as she laughed to calm the pain running through her body.

The nurse lowered the lights and told Michelle she needed to try and rest and explained to Xavier that he could stay within the room and showed him the pull-out sofa.

"The medications will help her rest," said the nurse.

Xavier pulled out his laptop and his information and wrote down every detail of the day and noted many events to include in his reporting once the investigation was complete. Xavier knew the incidents were sensitive, but the details needed to emerge to save others. After several hours of reviewing statements and audio footage, Xavier fell asleep within his chair.

"Xavier, Xavier," said Michelle in a weakened voice.

Xavier immediately jumped up and looked directly into Michelle's eyes and said, "You are mine, and I will never let anyone take you from me again. I want to spend the rest of my life with you, Michelle."

Michelle smiled and pulled his head to her chest and held him tightly to her body. "I thought I was never going to see you again, Xavier. I thought the barn was it, and my life was ending, but I fought with every ounce of energy, and now I'm here with you," said Michelle with watery eyes.

Michelle continued to hold him tight and said, "Is it over? What about the club?"

Xavier could hear the chatter of the police guard's radio who stationed out front but informed Michelle he did not know what was happening with the investigation now. Michelle asked Xavier to turn on the TV and see if there were any reports concerning the investigations. The media feed was silent concerning the ongoing situation. At the same time, Xavier explained to Michelle how the detective wanted him to hold off on his findings until they have secured the scene.

"Good morning, Michelle," said the doctor as he entered the room with a couple of nurses. "Sir, could you please step out for a few minutes to allow us time to examine Michelle's progress?" asked the doctor.

Xavier left the room and called the detective to see if there was any progress in determining the whereabouts of the people reported from Michelle who was held hostage in the building.

"Xavier, we appreciate everything you and Michelle have provided. Your information leads to us discovering more than twenty men and women being held captive in the building," explained the detective.

Xavier was pleased to hear law enforcement had raided the building and rescued many people. "However, we did not find the manager or person you and Michelle described as the 'bull,' but we have made several arrests with persons involved and have opened an active investigation into the organization and the ties to the string of murders. Your information saved a lot of lives today, Xavier," explained the detective.

"I cannot share too much information at this time, Xavier, but the inside of the building was like a torture chamber and filled with the presence of evil and pain," described Detective Swank. "The city is grateful for Michelle's courage and willingness to cooperate," said the detective.

"Thank you, Detective Swank. We look forward to working with you," said Xavier.

"You're most welcome, Xavier, but we must be mindful of the masterminds behind these events. They are still at large," explained the detective. "We also believe the deceased person named Carl might have been involved with orchestrating the events as well," said Detective Swank. "The more we investigate the scene, the more we are finding this operation was connected in a network of people and organizations. We must be careful as to what is reported to the people through the media, Xavier," said the detective.

CHAPTER 31

The doctor exited Michelle's room and called Xavier he could return and speak with Michelle. Xavier entered the room and found Michelle was sitting upright and looking much better.

"Well, hello, beautiful," said Xavier with a chirpy voice.

"Nice to see you, sexy man," said Michelle while displaying her crooked smile.

"There's my girl. I'm glad you're doing better and have some good news to share," said Xavier as he sat on the edge of Michelle's bedding. "The police found the club and saved many people, but they did not find the management of the organization or the person you described as the bull," said Xavier while holding Michelle's hand.

Michelle's eyes opened wide and looked as if she saw a ghost. "No, no, they have to find these guys. They will continue to hurt people," said Michelle in a desperate voice.

"They also believe Carl was tied deep within the organization and was a contributing factor within the club presence," said Xavier.

"Xavier, they're wrong! Carl was only a pawn and manipulated with sex rewards. They are pinning most of this on Carl to cover up their tracks," warned Michelle.

Xavier looked at Michelle and said, "The truth will be released very soon, and everyone will know what happened within that building and how it connected with a string of murders," explained Xavier.

"Xavier, I don't think everyone understands how complex this is and how the club had deep ties with persons of interest," said Michelle.

"The authorities will catch them, Michelle. You need to focus on resting and recovering," said Xavier.

"I'm sorry, they're still out there, and people are never going to be safe as long as they are here and using sex to control people," explained Michelle.

Xavier leaned forward and hugged Michelle while she pushed back with a painful grunt. "Sorry, that bastard Carl burned an image of a bullhead into my back, and it hurts badly," said Michelle.

Michelle covered her face once again with her hands and began to cry, saying, "I'm so messed up and ugly."

Xavier let out a low laugh while shaking his head and said, "Even with your hair a mess and underneath all these cuts and bruises, you are lovely, Michelle," said Xavier.

Michelle looked over Xavier's shoulder, turned the volume up on the TV, and listened as the media was live on the scene and reported the little bit of knowledge they had gained concerning the sex club while the building was on fire. They listened as the reporter revealed how multiple persons were rescued. While the investigation was continuing, a fire underneath the structure began to move upward and engulfed the scene into full flames.

"Brian, it appears our sources are reporting some kind of sex operation that is possibly tied to the recent murders. While we do not have all the details, local authorities are encouraging everyone to be mindful of the situation and stay away from this area for a while. We have received word that more than twenty people were rescued from bondage and several others arrested that are believed to be associated with this operation. It had come to our attention that others may have fled the scene before authorities could apprehend them. Still, detectives have assured us they are working diligently to track down the whereabouts of the persons involved. We know one local detective has been found deceased at the scene while another person of interest is being investigated. We are being told to fall back from the area due to the fire expanding more rapidly and have noticed the

Federal Bureau of Investigation has now taken over the scene. I'm Tammy Fellows, reporting live from Channel Seven News."

Michelle laid her hand onto Xavier's shoulder while muting the TV and said, "Thank you, the people needed to know the truth, and I'm forever grateful for you rescuing me."

Xavier kissed Michelle's hand and said, "That's what you do for people you love." Xavier could tell her he loved her a million times, but each time he repeated, Michelle felt as if it was the first time he said he loved her all over again.

"Oh, and the media had a special email filled with many details that will help inform the public," said Xavier as he smiled. Xavier's phone rang, and he stepped away to answer the call.

At the same time, Michelle overheard it was his place of work, congratulating him on his reporting, and asked him if he would release a detailed op-ed concerning the recent events that he will underwrite and would include his name as the subject matter expert. Xavier turned to Michelle and smiled but quickly felt his emotions fade when he caught sight of Michelle and her battered body.

"No, go, this is what you have worked so hard for. This is your time and chance to become who you are. We did this together," said Michelle.

"I can't leave you," said Xavier.

"You can, and you will. I'm fine, just hurry back later," said Michelle with an excited expression.

Xavier kissed Michelle, grabbed his gear, and headed out the door to pursue his office. He was going to accomplish his goals by writing how one brave woman brought down an entire sex cult while surviving death on many occasions. Michelle was saddened by the events but pleased Xavier was going to pursue his dream. She smiled and looked out the window as the clouds began to separate and rays of sunshine started to fill the room with light. Michelle felt the presence of a nurse entering her room who said, "Hey, Michelle, I need to examine your markings on your back."

Michelle sat up and allowed the nurse to open her hospital gown and pull back the bandaging. "Looks like someone wanted to send a message to you, Michelle, by marking your back," said the nurse.

Michelle thought the statement was odd but replied, "It was a horrific experience, something I do not want to talk about at this moment."

"The marking is beautiful. Just tell me, was he magnificent?" whispered the nurse.

"What? Who are you? Get the fuck away from me!" shouted Michelle.

The nurse covered Michelle's mouth tightly and ran her wet tongue up Michelle's face. "We know who you are and where you live and what you do. The bull will be waiting," said the nurse as she injected a sleeping agent into Michelle's IV.

"He gets what he wants, and he wants you," said the nurse into Michelle's ear.

Michelle's eyes became weak as her body gave in to the sleeping agent, falling into a deep sleep.

To be continued...

ABOUT THE AUTHOR

New author W. E. Rymer brings a whole new approach to erotic romance; erotic fantasy, the way it's supposed to be and without analogies or comparisons—just raw, descriptive, and filled with hot details. W. E. Rymer currently resides out of Nashville, Tennessee, while working in the health-care industry. I hope my direct and uncensored approach fulfills your desire for erotic fantasy.